FALLING THROUGH BLANKETS OF STARS

FALLING THROUGH BLANKETS OF STARS

KEITH MARCOTTI

This book is fiction, except for the parts that aren't.

Text copyright 2018 by Keith Marcotti

Cover art by Jeffrey Nguyen

paperback ISBN: 978-0-9998062-0-3
ebook ISBN: 978-0-9998062-1-0

Library of Congress control number: 2018903201

STONE**FOX**
PRESS

For my kids,
and for Matt.

King Sleep was father of a thousand sons—indeed a tribe—and of them all, the one he chose was Morpheus . . .

—OVID'S METAMORPHOSES, 8 AD

PROLOGUE

A T LAST, HE could return to the darkness.

Nox folded his wings and perched on the
stone windowsill. He squinted, peering through
the glass. In the center of the chamber, under gold-
en sheets, lay his prize.

Many slumbers ago—he'd lost count, it had
been so long—Nox had flown across the dark
lands of Nightmare and crossed into the wretched,
eternal daylight of Dream. His task was to find Asteria, where he would steal the girl and bring her
back to Nightmare as his prisoner—or die trying.

After weeks of searching in vain, he'd begun to
wonder if the castle Asteria—which was never in

the same place twice—would ever reveal itself to him. But today, as fate would have it, he'd been exploring a lightly wooded valley in the Mountains of Dream when the elusive structure happened to float directly overhead.

Asteria was a massive, sprawling complex of sloping white walls and spiraling white towers, its interior said to be a maze of cavernous ballrooms, throne rooms, courtyards, and secret passages, where unwelcome guests were meant to become lost forever.

After flying covertly through the light from window to window, carefully avoiding detection by any of the guards stationed along the castle walls, he'd at last found what he was looking for.

Without hesitation, he shattered the glass with his fist, spread his wings, and soared into the room.

The girl woke instantly. She screamed as Nox flew overhead, snatching her with a casual agility that betrayed his monstrous, misshapen form. She fought wildly to escape his grasp.

Without stopping, Nox tucked his wings, lowered his shoulder, and crashed through the glass of a window on the opposite side of the chamber, escaping into the open skies beyond with the writhing girl stowed firmly in his grip.

He was well aware of the weapons wielded by the famed Guardians of Asteria: the endless swords; golden blades fastened to the backplates of their golden armor. If one of these swords was removed from its sheath, an identical replacement would instantly appear in place of the last.

A group of guardians standing watch along the ramparts of a nearby wall burst into a frenzy when they spotted Nox fleeing, instantly unleashing a deadly barrage of swords, hurling them with unnatural speed. The weapons hissed by Nox on all sides, barely missing as he evaded, dipping and rolling.

A door by the guards suddenly burst open. A guardian emerged, this one taller than the others.

A leader, no doubt, his long, flowing hair uncon-cealed by a helmet. "Stop!" he yelled. "Hold your fire! It's taken the queen! If you miss, you could hit her! Get on the horses, hurry!"

Several silver, winged horses suddenly ap-peared behind the men on the wall. Their com-mander continued to shout orders, but his voice grew faint as Nox flew further from the floating castle, the whimpering girl's struggles weakening, subsiding.

THE NIGHTMARE KING sighed with impatience.

He sat on his throne, deep underground in the bowels of his castle, in a dark, cavernous dungeon. Before him, fading into the distant shadows, lay countless, towering rows of crudely stacked cages, each emitting the harmonious moaning and wail-ing of an unfortunate sleeper who'd found them-self locked within his personal prison; not one of the ignorant souls were even slightly aware that for them, this was only a dream.

A bad *dream*, he thought, with a small hint of amusement.

He simply wanted more. More sadness. More loneliness. More *suffering.* And that girl, the beautiful one who'd stolen his brother's heart, was the key to it all. In spite of all the time that had passed, he remained confident that Nox would eventually return with her.

Suddenly, the large wooden door set into the stone wall beside him began to creak open. The king sat up, leaning forward, watching eagerly.

A moment later, he smiled with relief. His long wait had at last come to an end.

There, in the torch-lit hallway, stood his faithful servant; the phantom known as Nox. He was truly a gruesome sight to behold. Black from head to toe, four bulbous eyeballs lining his brow, and a mouthful of protruding, jagged teeth. His wings and hulking, muscular frame did not reflect light of any kind, giving him the overall appearance of a living, breathing shadow.

The girl struggled desperately in the monster's grip, her silver gown thoroughly torn and smudged with filth—no doubt the result of her struggles with the unrelenting Nox.

"Where have you taken me?" she demanded. "What do you want from me? What is this place?"

NOX TUCKED HIS wings and slumped forward through the doorway. He approached his king's throne and threw the girl carelessly onto the stone floor.

"It is done," he growled.

His master, who could change form at will and take any shape he desired—both large and small—was currently little more than black mist with a vaguely human silhouette, accented by two red, glowing eyes.

"You cannot do this!" shouted the girl in defiance, climbing to her feet.

The Nightmare King's sudden laughter echoed throughout the vast chamber. Nearby torches lining the walls flickered and danced, cowering and shrinking away from the repulsive sound.

Tears formed in the girl's eyes, but she stood her ground.

The king's shifting, dark figure slowly raised an arm, pointing toward a large opening in the ground by his throne.

Without a word, Nox approached the girl, picked her up, and carried her to the side of the pit. Her eyes grew wide with fear as she looked into the bubbling, black water of the gateway below.

"No! Please, no!" she pleaded, kicking and punching wildly at Nox's arms and chest.

He tossed her in.

She screamed as she fell, and Nox watched her tumble through the air, shiny dress and red hair flowing as she kicked her legs and flailed her arms.

There was a bright green flash of light as she hit the water, and the screaming stopped.

The red-haired girl was gone.

THE NIGHTMARE KING sat back, satisfied. That little scene had been quite amusing. The girl was more beautiful than he'd imagined; his pathetic brother would surely do anything to recover such a creature as that. And with Morpheus gone, Dream would be left completely defenseless.

And then, he thought, a greedy smile slithering across his face, *all of Sleep—both Nightmare* and *Dream—will be mine until the end of time.*

I

"WHA-HUH? WHAT'S ... WHAT?" mumbled confused, half-asleep Ashlynne. As she looked up at her twin brother Julian through fuzzy morning-eyes, she could see that he looked extra happy for some reason. His mop of blonde hair was all messed up from sleeping, but his light-blue eyes were wide with excitement.

"Wake up!" he shouted, from roughly two inches away. "I just heard Grammy talking to Mom downstairs. We finally get to see what the cake looks like!" Unable to contain himself, he sprinted out of the room and down the stairs.

Ashlynne raised her head—which took considerable effort at the moment—and looked around the messy bedroom, which was currently bathing in the bright July sunlight that poured in through the open windows. She was slowly becoming used to the idea of getting up and out of bed when Julian's words suddenly sank in; Grammy was downstairs, and she'd brought a cake. And with that, the cobwebs lifted from Ashlynne's sleepy mind, and she remembered. Today was the day of their annual birthday cookout.

Every kid in their fourth-grade class had been given an invitation on the last day of school a couple of weeks earlier, and she hoped that at least some of them would show up. It was summertime, after all, and you never knew who would be out of town on vacation with their family.

Each year, Ashlynne's grandmother—who owned a popular, nationwide chain of bakeries—would promise to make her and Julian a birthday cake, but every time, something would come up and she'd cancel, and they'd wind up with some lame cupcakes from the supermarket as a last-minute replacement. Grammy had been telling them for weeks that this year, for their tenth birthday, she would at last fulfill her promise with an extra-special cake. Ashlynne was skeptical, but had decided to give her grandmother the benefit of the doubt. Maybe she'd finally come through.

OUTSIDE IN THE backyard, under the hot morning sun, Julian stood next to the cake his grandmother arrived with. After his parents had transported it from the bed of Grammy's pickup truck to where it currently rested on the grass in a large, silver tray the size of a bathtub, his father had walked next door to ask their new neighbor, Mr. Morfy—who'd just moved in a couple of months earlier—if they could borrow his picnic table to display it.

The cake—which had been shaped as a pirate ship—was massive, with cannons sticking out the sides, a plank for the bad guys to walk, a huge white sail, and fastened to the main mast was a black flag bearing the famous skull-and-crossbones pirate symbol. It looked so real that Julian couldn't believe it was actually a cake.

His father and Mr. Morfy returned together carrying the picnic table and placed it on the cement patio behind the deep end of the swimming pool. Then the two men walked over to the cake, bent low, and lifted it off the grass.

"Can we really eat that whole thing?" Julian asked.

"Of course, buddy," his father answered, grunting under the weight of the cake. "Everything except the sails and the flag." He and Mr. Morfy carefully made their way over to the patio and lowered the cake down onto the table.

Julian's mouth began to water. He hadn't eaten any breakfast yet, and now all he could think about was eating cake. His stomach growled.

His thoughts of food vanished as a sudden squeal of brakes drew his attention, and he turned to find a big, brightly painted van pulling up in front of the house. There were words written in colorful letters on the side of the van, but he was too far away from the street to read what they said.

"What's that?" he asked.

His father looked up and smiled when he saw the truck. "Surprise," he said. "I ordered you and your sister one of those giant inflatable bouncy houses for your party today. I picked the one that looks like a castle. I hope that's okay."

Julian couldn't believe what he was hearing. Bouncy houses were pretty close to the top of his private list of favorite things.

"Aaah!" was all he could manage, and he took off running in search of his sister. She was missing *everything*.

ASHLYNNE HAD NEVER been much of a morning person. At least fifteen minutes had passed, she guessed, since Julian had woken her—and here she was, still upstairs, attempting to will herself up and out of bed.

Suddenly she heard Julian yelling from the backyard. She rolled out of bed and shuffled to the window, just in time to see him running across the grass toward the house.

She plopped down on the small rug next to the window and began to pull on her slippers. A moment later she heard the screen door downstairs slam shut as Julian's feet pounded across the floor below, coming to a halt near the bottom of the stairs.

"Ashlynne!" he yelled up to her. "You have to wake up! Dad ordered us a bouncy house! Hurry, you *gotta* come see!" His feet thundered across the floor again, in the opposite direction this time, the door slamming once more as he ran back outside.

Ashlynne finished pulling on her slippers then

stood up, yawning and stretching. She strolled to her bedside table, picked up a brush, and began the grueling task of combing her long brown hair.

Today it was particularly tangled. As she brushed through the mess, wincing in pain, she could hear Julian laughing and yelling while he ran around outside. He was so lucky. His hair was so short that he never had to worry about it at all. She finished brushing, put her hair up into a ponytail, and went downstairs.

A FEW HOURS later, most of the guests had arrived.

In need of a short break from playing with her friends, Ashlynne grabbed a drink and a bowl of potato chips, then sat down on one of the many lawn chairs surrounding the pool. Her entire family was there in the backyard, along with all the kids that she and her brother had invited from school, who'd each brought their respective parents and brothers and sisters.

Their pretty teacher, red-haired Ms. Aarya, had also been invited, but she'd called yesterday afternoon to say she wouldn't be able to attend. But it seemed like practically everyone else Ashlynne had ever met was there celebrating. Even Uncle Charlie.

Uncle Charlie had arrived late, with droopy eyes and messy hair, but at least his t-shirt had a picture of a bow tie on it, which was apparently Uncle Charlie's way of looking fancy. After mumbling a brief "happy birthday" to Ashlynne and Julian, he'd sprawled out on a big lawn chair by the pool and gone to sleep, sweating profusely, his fat, hairy stomach hanging out the bottom of his t-shirt as he snored away under the hot sun. Occasionally he'd reach up to scratch at his bushy, tangled beard.

Uncle Charlie didn't know it, but he was currently being watched.

For some time now, Ashlynne had been keeping an eye on Mr. Fuzzybottom, the family cat, who'd most likely been awake all night long doing cat-related things, and was probably long overdue for some sleep. He'd been secretly watching all the guests arrive from where he lurked in the shadows beneath the row of large bushes that ran alongside the back of the house. But now that Uncle Charlie was here sleeping, Fuzzy was clearly stalking his prey, head low and butt sticking up, tail slowly swaying as he patiently waited for the right moment to strike.

It didn't take long. Two or three minutes later, Mr. Fuzzybottom emerged from his hiding place and crept slowly across the freshly cut grass. When he reached the lawn chair, he hopped onto uncle Charlie's chest. Uncle Charlie stirred slightly, but did not wake; Fuzzy was a considerably small cat, and very light, possessing almost ninja-like abilities. After a moment of intense stillness and staring, Fuzzy went for it. Very gently, one paw at a time, he stepped onto Uncle Charlie's head, curled up, and closed his eyes.

Ashlynne laughed. "Julian, Jacob, look! Fuzzy's sleeping on Uncle Charlie's head!"

"Hang on a second!" called Julian from the opposite side of the pool. The bouncy house was currently unavailable due to the large volume of waist-high children in attendance, so he'd begun skateboarding at the end of the driveway with his friend Jacob, the two of them practicing tricks on Julian's quarter-pipe ramp. Julian expertly kick-flipped his skateboard off the deck of the ramp, landing on the smooth, flat-ground cement beside it, where he turned sideways and skidded to a stop. He stepped off the board, snapped it with his toe so it popped into the air, then caught it with one hand. Jacob clapped as Julian bowed dramatically, then they both looked over at Fuzzy and laughed.

Sleeping on people's heads was something that Mr. Fuzzybottom was quite fond of. Over the years, the family had taken to keeping their bedroom doors closed while they slept, as a precaution.

WHEN IT CAME time to open presents, everyone except for the sleeping Uncle Charlie was crowded around Ashlynne and Julian as they tore through their gifts. No one seemed to notice Louie, Mr. Morfy's Pomeranian puppy, as he crawled under the fence and into the yard through a hole he'd dug earlier that morning.

As Louie snuck through the big backyard, he followed his nose to a huge something that sat on top of a table next to the giant water hole. He jumped up onto the table and licked his lips, preparing to sink his teeth into whatever this deliciously-scented thing was.

JULIAN WAS IN the middle of unwrapping a mysteriously pointy-looking gift when he happened to look past the crowd of people surrounding him, and was a bit surprised to see Louie standing on the plank of his birthday cake. As the little dog slowly opened his mouth to take a bite, Grammy suddenly screamed "My cake!" and took off running, straight for Louie and the cake.

"Get away!" she yelled as she ran, flailing her arms like a madwoman. "Get away from there!"

Julian had never seen his grandmother move so fast before.

Louie, apparently startled by all the sudden noise, jumped then landed back on the plank of the ship so hard it broke off, catapulting a rather large piece of cake through the air.

On the other side of the yard, Uncle Charlie was still snoring away in his lawn chair with Mr. Fuzzybottom curled up on his head. At that moment, he happened to be in the midst of a long, loud snore when the piece of cake Louie had sent flying landed directly in his open mouth. He sat up immediately and spat out the cake, jolting Fuzzy out of a deep sleep. The cat leapt forward off his head, directly into the path of Grammy who was still yelling and running toward the cake. They collided, and the flying Mr. Fuzzybottom wrapped his limbs around Grammy's head, hissing and wailing in terror. Grammy continued onward at full speed, arms outstretched, apparently unable to see now that Fuzzy was attached.

When he saw Grammy coming for him, Louie hopped down from the table and ran.

Poor Louie, thought Julian, his furry little friend clearly frightened.

A moment later, Grammy ran straight into the old, brittle wooden table, and it toppled helplessly into the water along with the cake, Grammy, and Mr. Fuzzybottom.

"Hey look, it floats!" yelled Julian's cousin Ava, pointing toward the cake, its large sails catching the warm summer breeze as it braved the waters of the pool.

The party erupted into laughter.

A moment later, Julian's father came to the rescue. He jumped in and helped Grammy out of the water, then removed the wet, shivering Mr. Fuzzybottom from her head.

As soon as his paws touched the ground, the cat bolted across the grass. Normally he avoided dogs, but he scurried under the fence and disappeared into Mr. Morfy's yard, right behind the fleeing Louie.

"Fuzzy no, wait!" said Ashlynne, who'd been standing next to Julian as they watched the action unfold. She frowned. "I hope he comes home before it gets dark out."

"He always comes back," said Julian. "Don't worry."

Mr. Fuzzybottom would be fine. At the moment, Julian had more important things to worry about. He sat down and resumed opening his birthday presents.

LATER THAT DAY, after the guests had all left and the pool was cleaned up, Ashlynne was sitting in the backyard with her brother, inspecting their mountain of gifts. There were action figures, dolls, a whole stack of video games, skateboards—one for each of them—and so much more. There was so much stuff, Ashlynne didn't know what to do first.

"I hope you guys had fun at your party, and sorry about Louie!"

She looked up and saw the very tall Mr. Morfy standing on his back porch, holding Louie. He gave Ashlynne and Julian a big wave. He was a nice man, but always seemed sort of sad.

"It's okay!" she said, at the same exact time as Julian. She and her brother frequently responded to people simultaneously. It was almost never on purpose.

Mr. Morfy smiled half heartedly then rustled

his puppy's fur between the ears. "Well, I guess I'll see you guys later. Happy birthday!" Then he turned and walked into his house.

II

LATER THAT NIGHT, Julian and his sister were in their room. They were supposed to be in their beds, sleeping.

Julian, however, was sitting in his favorite chair in his favorite corner, playing one of his new video games. Ashlynne was on the opposite side of the room, by the window next to her bed. For quite some time now she'd been looking out toward Mr. Morfy's house with her arms folded in front of her chest.

Julian didn't understand why she was so worried. Mr. Fuzzybottom was always going outside, and he always came back home sooner or later.

"He's never been gone this long before," said Ashlynne, as if she'd known what Julian was thinking, "and he always comes back before the sun goes down. Julian, come here and look. There's a basement window open over at Mr. Morfy's house. I bet that's where Fuzzy's hiding."

Julian sighed and paused his game. He put down the controller, stood up and stretched, then approached the window.

"See?" she said, pointing. "I *know* that's where he went. The window's probably too high for him to jump back out. And look; there's a light on in there. It looks like one of those black lights Uncle Charlie has in his basement."

Julian had noticed the dull blue light glowing in their neighbor's basement window before, and had wondered what might be its source. "Well, why don't we go over and look inside?"

Ashlynne looked at him, eyebrows raised. "Are you serious? You want to go down there?" She looked back out the window and shook her head. "No way. It's really late, and Mom and Dad are already in bed. If we get caught, we'll be in trouble."

"It'll be okay," he said, in what he hoped was a convincing tone. "We'll just have to be really quiet." He wasn't too worried about their cat; Mr. Fuzzybottom could take care of himself. Julian was curious about that blue light. It looked like light reflecting off the surface of water, sort of glimmering, sort of moving. Maybe Mr. Morfy was keeping some type of illegal shark in a tank down there or something. Plus, sneaking out when they were supposed to be in bed sleeping was an exciting idea. He and Ashlynne had never done something like that before.

Ashlynne looked at him and frowned. "Okay," she said timidly. "I guess."

They each grabbed a pair of sneakers and crept barefoot into the dark hall. Their parents' room was a couple of doors down, in the opposite direction of the stairway. Quickly and quietly, Julian led the way to the stairs and descended.

Once they were safely in the kitchen, they each sat on the cool hardwood floor and slipped on their shoes.

Julian grabbed a flashlight from the junk drawer next to the refrigerator, figuring he might need it in Mr. Morfy's basement; the blue light that was on down there didn't look very bright, and Fuzzy might be hiding in a dark corner, if he was even hiding down there at all.

He looked at Ashlynne. "You ready?"

"I guess so," she whispered. She looked nervous.

"Okay, then let's go." Julian walked to the back door and unlocked it. He gripped the knob with a sweaty palm and pulled the door open slowly, his heart pounding, making as little noise as possible, then slipped outside as the grassy, humid scent of the hot summer night invaded his senses.

Ashlynne followed and closed the door behind them.

Julian led the way across the backyard grass under the light of the full moon. He approached the fence that separated their yard from Mr. Morfy's and clicked on the flashlight, scanning the ground until he spotted the hole that Louie had dug earlier to sneak into their yard. He clicked off the flashlight. It was a pretty deep hole, definitely big enough for him and Ashlynne to crawl under one at a time.

Julian dropped to the ground, wriggled under the fence, then propped himself up on his knees as he scanned foreign territory. It looked like the coast was clear. Ashlynne crawled through a moment later and climbed to her feet. He stood up next to her, then together they approached the open basement window, dropped to their knees, and looked inside. Julian could see immediately where the light was coming from.

There was a wooden box against the far wall of the largely empty basement room. It looked very old, sort of like a treasure chest from a pirate movie. Its lid was being held slightly open by something, like a suitcase with too much clothing stuffed inside.

Whatever was in the box looked to be covered in some type of glitter. The mysterious contents shimmered and shined, and was clearly the cause of the light they'd seen from their bedroom window.

"What *is* that, in that box?" Julian spoke as quietly as he could.

"I don't know," said Ashlynne. "Do you see Fuzzy anywhere in there?"

Julian clicked on the flashlight and aimed it into the basement, shining it into all the dark corners where the cat might be hiding. Sure enough, after searching for a moment, he spotted the grey cat cowering beneath the stairway.

"There he is!" Ashlynne whispered. "I was right! It must be too high for him to jump back out on his own."

"I guess I'll go in and get him."

"Julian, no! We know he's in there, we know he's okay. We'll just come back tomorrow and ring Mr. Morfy's doorbell and tell him we think our cat's in his basement. We can't go in there!"

Julian shook his head. "No way. You can stay out here. I have to see what's in that box, glowing like that."

Ashlynne grimaced. "You're crazy. You're gonna get us in trouble."

But Julian was already on his belly, sliding into the open window feet first. "I'll be right back." He looked up at her, grinning. "It'll be alright."

A moment later his feet collided with the cement floor of the musty basement. An echo resounded, sending Julian's heart into a renewed flurry. He took a deep breath, listening for any hint of a sound upstairs, not moving a muscle. When he heard nothing, he hurried over to Mr. Fuzzybottom and scooped him up, dutifully handed the meowing cat out the window to Ashlynne, then approached the wooden box and knelt before it.

Julian carefully lifted the lid, squinting as the bluish-white light poured out. He reached into the box and pulled out a pair of blankets, or sheets, or possibly even curtains, he guessed. Whatever they were, they were black, and soft as silk. Softer even, somehow. And covered with blue and white glitter.

But this was no ordinary glitter.

He grabbed one of the blankets by the corners and held it up, spreading it as wide as he could. He couldn't make any sense of it; as he looked at the blanket, he got the sense that he was looking through a window, at stars in the sky. But it was no sky he had ever seen before. There were way too many stars.

Without thinking twice, he crumpled the blankets into a ball and ran to the window. "Ashlynne, take these, hurry!"

She looked at him like he'd just grown several extra heads. "What? No way! Julian, put those back! We got Fuzzy, let's just get out of here!"

There was no time to argue. He *had* to show these things to his friend Jacob. He could sneak back in here and return the blankets tomorrow night, before Mr. Morfy even noticed they were gone.

Julian slid a wooden chair to the window, stepped onto it, stuffed the blankets out onto the grass, then reached up and pulled himself out.

He climbed to his feet, grabbed the blankets, then sprinted straight for the hole under the fence. He dropped to his knees, shoving the blankets through to the other side. Then he pulled himself through with Ashlynne close behind, whispering in protest.

They snuck back into the house and up to their bedroom without waking their parents, then collapsed onto their beds, breathless and sweating.

After a minute or two, as the adrenaline wore off and his heartbeat slowed to a normal rhythm, Julian's eyes grew heavy.

Before long, he was fast asleep.

III

ASHLYNNE KNEW SHE was dreaming. She didn't always know it when she was dreaming, but it happened sometimes.

She was in her backyard. Her father was cooking on his grill, and her mother was busy digging in the garden.

The two strange blankets that Julian had taken from Mr. Morfy's basement were floating on the surface of the pool. Ashlynne was bouncing on one of the blankets, and Julian was next to her, bouncing on the other, as if the blankets were trampolines. She briefly wondered if she and her brother were sharing a dream again, which was something else that happened sometimes.

She and Julian bounced higher and higher together, each bounce higher than the last, until they were eventually bouncing all the way up into the clouds. They laughed and yelled out silly things, blindly accepting the unusual nature of what was happening, as dreamers do. Mom and Dad didn't appear concerned, either. They just kept on doing their grilling and digging like everything was normal, as if their high-bouncing children—who could possibly collide with an unsuspecting airplane at any moment—were not in any immediate danger.

Just then, as they made their way back down to the pool after a particularly high bounce, the blankets waiting below began to glow.

The moment Ashlynne's feet touched the glowing blanket, there was a blinding flash of light, and she fell straight through.

She then found herself surrounded by a countless number of tiny twinkling lights. It was like she was inside a huge snow globe full of little Christmas lights instead of snow. Some of the lights were close, some were far away, and some were in between. Beyond was nothing but black.

As Ashlynne inspected her surroundings, she began to feel as if a dense fog was slowly being lifted from her mind. She could see Julian floating nearby, only about an arm's length away. It looked like he was trying to speak, but no voice was coming out.

"Julian!" she called. It was like trying to yell underwater; her voice hardly made a sound.

The surrounding lights began to grow, fusing together as colors slowly emerged, and then suddenly Ashlynne and her brother were surrounded by a blue sky.

A sudden wind rushed up from beneath to greet them, and they were falling once more.

"Julian!" screamed Ashlynne. Her voice seemed to work correctly now. "Where are we?" Julian wasn't crying, but it looked like he was about to start any second.

"I don't know!" he answered, eyes wide, the wind tossing his hair in every direction.

Ashlynne caught sight of the two sparkling blankets off in the distance, fluttering away in the strong wind. A moment later they disappeared from view entirely.

Below was what appeared to be a solid layer of clouds stretching as far as she could see in every direction. It reminded her of being on an airplane on a cloudy day, when the plane flies so high that it breaks through the clouds and you find yourself on an otherworldly landscape of white.

Only these clouds, if they were in fact clouds, were not white at all. Instead, they appeared to be just about every color possible *except* white, all blended together in mesmerizing, swirling patterns.

And the other difference, Ashlynne noticed as a chill rolled up her spine, was that though it appeared to be daytime, there was no sun. Anywhere.

"Julian, are those clouds down there?"

"Aaaaaah!" said Julian, apparently too frightened to provide a coherent answer.

Ashlynne screamed along with him as they plummeted together, rocketing downward. At the last moment before reaching the surface of the colorful clouds, she closed her eyes, bracing herself. She really hoped these were clouds.

When she opened her eyes, safely through the layer of what were indeed clouds, there was so much going on around her and Julian that she forgot all about being in mortal danger, if only for a brief moment.

The sky was crowded with hundreds, if not thousands of people, both old and young, all flying around. But they weren't flying in airplanes or helicopters.

It was insane. She felt like she was in the middle of one of those Where's Waldo pictures, where a thousand things are happening all at once, and Waldo is hiding somewhere in the craziness. She was speechless. It couldn't be real.

A group of kids zoomed past on what appeared to be hover boards—not the recent products notorious for spontaneous combustion, but the wheel-less, floating skateboards of the future—and they seemed to be having a great time. Some of the people rode broomsticks. Others were flying around like superman, wearing costumes complete with capes. There were entire swarms of UFOs and flying cars, people riding flying carpets and dragons of every size and color imaginable . . . the list went on and on, each aviator even stranger than the last. And somehow, although the sky was so thoroughly crowded, nothing was colliding. It was like some enormous choreographed scene from a movie, everything flowing together in harmony.

And behind the chaos, far in the distance, was a large, white castle, floating through the sky. Ashlynne shook her head. *Where are we?*

She and Julian fell like rocks, straight through

the impossible scene, narrowly avoiding a collision every two or three seconds.

Ashlynne could see water far below—a huge lake, or perhaps even an ocean. She quickly realized that unless she or Julian managed to find a couple of parachutes within the next fifteen seconds or so, they would almost certainly be killed.

And another problem was that Ashlynne couldn't make any sense of the way she *felt*. She'd woken from the middle of a dream many times before, usually to the unpleasant sound of their mother yelling about being late for school. She knew what it felt like to wake up from being asleep, and that was how she felt now. Only she was not in her bed where she should be.

Luckily, Julian was still only about an arm's length away. "Julian!" she yelled. "Where are we? Are we sharing a dream again?"

He looked at her like she was crazy. "Who cares? We're gonna die!"

Ashlynne focused her thoughts. Suddenly, she

had an idea.

"Help!" she yelled. "Please, help us! Someone, please!" She hoped that maybe one of the flying cars would catch them, or maybe one of the people on broomsticks. She wasn't picky. She'd be happy if a person on a flying cactus caught them. But none of the people seemed to notice her. Either none of them could hear her, or they just didn't care.

"What is that down there?" She pointed toward a large, dark shape on the water's surface almost directly under them.

Julian scanned the water below, squinting. "I can't really tell from way up here, but I think it's a ship!"

"Well whatever it is, if we don't think of something soon, we're gonna land right on top of it!"

They continued their plummet, screaming and yelling like mad as the ship grew steadily closer, and closer . . . at the very last moment, a pair of people in superhero costumes suddenly swooped in, plucked Ashlynne and Julian out of the air, gracefully placed them onto the wooden deck of the pirate ship, then flew away without a word.

"HAH!" Julian said, grinning. "I can't believe it! We're okay!"

Ashlynne looked up and tried to spot their two saviors, who'd disappeared into the crowded skies above. "Thank you!" she called out cheerfully. She hoped they could somehow hear her.

"Thank you!" said Julian, following her lead.

A group of small men gathered on the deck. There were maybe twenty of them, all roughly the same height as Ashlynne and her brother, dressed in tattered, filthy clothes that appeared to have been stitched together sometime back in the seventeenth century. Many of them had piercings in their noses, eyebrows, and ears, and several wore eye patches. Each had drawn a cutlass-shaped sword, except for one near the back, who apparently had no sword. He seemed to be trying hard to look extra mean.

"Who are you guys?" Julian asked them. "And where are we?"

One of the men stepped forward. He wore a black bandana and a long, dark green jacket covered with patches and medals.

"We're currently in Dream," he said, his accent thick, "and we are the Leprechauns." He gestured to the men behind him. "And in case you were wonderin' who I am . . ." He slid the sword he'd been holding into the sheath at his side and grinned. Ashlynne noticed that at least half of his teeth were gold. "I'm the captain of this ship."

The captain had just finished speaking when one of the men behind him suddenly dropped his sword and began to snore. The snoring man wore two eye patches—one covering each eye, an ornately stitched image of a golden eyeball adorning the center of each patch—and he'd apparently fallen asleep while standing up. The other men ignored him.

Ashlynne giggled, then quickly covered her

mouth with her hand. She didn't want to offend anyone.

The captain glanced over his shoulder, then looked back to Ashlynne and Julian. "That's Jerry," he informed them. "He's blind. And he likes to sleep. Now please tell me somethin'—if you don't mind me askin'—who are you two, and why are you on my ship?"

Julian just looked at her and shrugged, so Ashlynne decided to answer for them. "I'm Ashlynne, and this is my brother, Julian." She frowned. "I'm sorry, but I'm not sure why we're on your ship. We were falling, and then those two nice people flew in and saved us—"

"We don't even know how we got here," Julian interrupted, " . . . wherever here is. And if you guys are leprechauns, then why are you all dressed like pirates?"

The captain looked at Julian and raised an eyebrow. "Have you ever seen a real leprechaun before, lad?"

"Well, no," mumbled Julian.

"How about a real pirate? Ever seen one of those?"

Julian shook his head.

"Then how do you presume to know what they dress like?" pressed the captain.

"Well . . . I guess I don't." Julian looked down. His cheeks turned red.

Ashlynne smiled. The little guy had him there.

"I can assure you, my boy, we are indeed leprechauns," said the captain.

Julian turned to Ashlynne. "He does talk like one. Maybe they really are leprechauns."

Ashlynne rolled her eyes. "How do *you* know what a leprechaun talks like?"

"I've seen that cereal commercial with the leprechaun, like, a million times," Julian said, matter-of-factly.

Ashlynne shook her head. "This is crazy. Are we sharing a dream again?" she asked him, but quickly realized that there would be no way to be sure until she woke up.

Ashlynne always remembered everything she dreamt about once she woke up, and sometimes Julian would be in her dreams. And every once in a while, he would wake up and tell her about having the exact same dream, *before* she'd tell him about *her* dream. So this could either be a dream version of Julian or the real Julian. She'd have to wait until morning to find out.

Julian swiped his hair out of his eyes. "I don't know. I mean, I think so, but this is all really weird, even for a dream. Everything seems way too . . . *real*, or something. I feel like I already woke up. But this is definitely a dream." He looked up, toward the sky full of people, and slowly shook his head. "It *has* to be."

"I wonder if this has anything to do with those weird glowing blankets you took from Mr. Morfy's basement," said Ashlynne. "I think I saw them up there in the sky with us. The wind blew them really far away."

"Excuse me," the captain said, stepping closer. "What was that you were just sayin' about glowin' blankets?"

⬖

ASHLYNNE TOLD THE captain the story of how Julian had taken the blankets from Mr. Morfy's basement. When she finished, the little man grimaced and slapped himself on the forehead with his palm.

"Don't you two realize what you've done?" he asked them.

Both Ashlynne and Julian stared, expressionless. "No," they answered, at the same time.

"You've taken the Blankets of Stars from King Morpheus, and now he's got no way to return!"

Julian's eyes widened. "King Morpheus? What do you mean? We took those from our neighbor, Mr. Morfy."

"Don't you see?" the captain shot back, face

reddening. "The Blankets of Stars belong to King Morpheus. They're the only two in existence. If you have them, you took them from him. Morfy is clearly just a cover name!"

Julian turned to Ashlynne. "I always thought that was a weird name."

Ashlynne couldn't believe what she was hearing. "Mr. Morfy is a *king*? No way!"

The little man took a deep breath, apparently attempting to calm down. He began pacing back and forth before his men. "Yes way, my lady. And I'm afraid those blankets your brother took from him were his only way of returnin' here to us. Without his Blankets of Stars, he'll be just like all the other sleepers—he won't stay long, and he won't notice nothin' except his own dream." He stopped pacing and fixed them with a stern look. "This is a very serious situation for the two of you," he said, a knobby finger outstretched. "I'm afraid that unless you're a sleeper, the only way to travel between here and the Real World is by fallin' asleep under those blankets. Unless, of course, you go to Nightmare and use one of their ways," he added with a feigned shiver.

"But wait a second," said Ashlynne, "we didn't fall asleep under the blankets...unless either Mom or Dad came in to check on us, and covered us up with them."

"So does that mean we're stuck here, in a dream, *forever?*" asked Julian.

"No, you aren't *having* a dream," the captain explained softly. "You're awake, here, *in* Dream."

"What do you mean, *in* Dream?" Ashlynne didn't understand.

The captain shook his head. He turned, facing his men. "Alright lads, back to what you were doin'!" he growled.

As the other leprechauns—who were all very much dressed as pirates—began to wander away, the captain strolled to the rail of the ship, then gestured to Ashlynne and Julian to do the same. They approached and stood beside him, Ashlynne resting her elbows on the polished wooden railing.

The captain cleared his throat. "There be two places, as far as I know," he said. "First, there's the Real World, where the sleepers live—where you two came from. And then there's Sleep, the place of dreams and nightmares.

"Within the realm of Sleep, there be two domains: Dream, and Nightmare. This is a part of Dream, where we are now. And then there's Nightmare; a dark place that lies beyond the dreamlands."

"So," said Julian, "that means when we go to sleep at night, if we have a dream—or a nightmare—we actually go to a place called Sleep?"

"Yes, lad," said the captain. "Dream is where sleepers wind up when they're havin' a good dream, and Nightmare is where they find themselves durin' a bad dream."

Ashlynne was surprised that dreams worked that way. But she had to admit, if it was true, it actually made a lot of sense.

"So all those people flying around up there," she said, gesturing toward the sky, "they're all having dreams?"

The captain glanced up. "Yep. But they don't often pay attention to much, other than what they're dreamin' about."

"Then what happens *after* someone dreams about something?" Ashlynne asked. "I mean, if I dreamed about riding a horse, would the horse just disappear when I woke up?"

"Oh no, very much the opposite," he explained. "The sleepers do indeed disappear when they wake up. I've seen it happen many times with my own eyes. But whatever places or things they dream about remain here, forever. That's how everything in Sleep is created, you see. Even us leprechauns. We were dreamt of long ago by an adventurous young lad. That's how we got here."

Julian grinned. "Really? Everything we've ever dreamed about is still here somewhere? That's awesome!"

The captain squinted at him. "Aye, lad. Awesome at times, perhaps. But the trouble is, the same rules apply in Nightmare, which lies all around us. Folks dream up all sorts of terrible things there, in that dark place. Sometimes those things sneak into Dream and give us all sorts of trouble." He frowned. "See, Dream is ruled over by King Morpheus, the protector of dreams, while his brother—who's thoroughly evil, mind you—rules over Nightmare. No one knows the brother's true name, so we just call him the Nightmare King.

"Basically, this whole thing in a nutshell is that Morpheus has always been here to protect us from whatever the Nightmare King sends our way; but now, thanks to you two and your thievery, Morpheus is unable to return." He eyed them both. "Okay, here's the plan. You two aren't sleepers; you're quite clearly awake. And you apparently got here using the blankets. That means the blankets are in Sleep somewhere, most likely here in

Dream, like you. So we need to find them. Because without those blankets, you'll both be stuck here, and Morpheus'll have no way of returnin' to protect us."

"Wait . . . we'll be *stuck* here?" asked Ashlynne, panic suddenly gripping her. "There's no other way to get home without the blankets?"

The captain paused, as if considering something. "Unfortunately, no," he said, after a moment. "Not without venturin' into Nightmare. But it'd be quite an easy thing to do if you still had the blankets with you. You'd just have to cover yourselves up with 'em and fall asleep. Then you'd wake up in the Real World, I suppose wherever you came from in the first place. All you'd have to do then would be return the blankets to the king. It'd be quite simple, really."

"Then we need to find the blankets!" said Ashlynne. "I want to go home!"

IV

ASHLYNNE WAS SITTING on the deck of the ship, her back resting against the base of the main mast. She hugged her bent legs while resting her forehead on her knees, hiding her face. She didn't want to talk to anyone. She just wanted to go home.

The unexpected sound of barking startled her, and she looked up through tearful eyes as a small dog came running from somewhere out of sight, its fur all white except for a patch of black over its left eye. The dog immediately approached Julian, who still stood at the ship's railing with the captain, and began jumping up and down next to him, emitting little yelps as its tail wagged into a blur.

Julian put his hands up, defending himself from the dog's enthusiastic greeting. "What's its name?"

"This be Stewie the Dog," the captain said with an amused smile. "And by the looks of it, he's found a new friend."

"I think he likes you, Julian," said Ashlynne, wiping away tears with the back of her hand.

Stewie flopped onto his back, tongue lolling out to the side. Julian knelt and began scratching the little dog's stomach. "It's going to be okay, Ashlynne," he said as he scratched. "We'll find those blankets and get back home. I know we will."

Ashlynne wanted so badly to believe that, but she wasn't so sure. Her eyes began to well up with fresh tears. "How do you know?"

He didn't answer right away. "I guess I don't know," he said a moment later. "But I do know that if we just sit around worrying and crying, we'll never get home."

Ashlynne tucked some of her long hair behind her ear, rested her head back against the mast, and closed her eyes. She took a deep breath, doing her best to focus her thoughts on the sensation of her breath, slowly inhaling and exhaling, just as her father had taught her to do when she was upset about something.

Julian was right. Sitting here and feeling sorry for herself wouldn't help them find those blankets, and she wanted to go home. She opened her eyes and nodded. "I'm sorry Julian. You're right. We'll get through this. We have to."

SEVERAL MINUTES LATER, Julian stood with Ashlynne at the ship's helm. The captain, who'd taken over for the previous helmsman, whistled an unfamiliar tune as he spun the wheel left and right, guiding the way. The three of them had run out of things to talk about and were silently watching the myriad of strange dreams that flew above and around the ship.

Julian could see land far in the distance; the leprechaun's ship appeared to be floating in the center of an enormous, circular lake.

His gaze was drawn to a section of land, maybe four or five miles wide, he guessed, full of towering, curling roller coasters. After a moment of inspection, he realized that a bunch of waterslides were mixed in too.

To the immediate left of the roller coasters was a city that looked like it belonged on another planet. The familiar, rectangular-shaped skyscrapers Julian was accustomed to were accompanied by a scattering of the strangest structures he'd ever laid eyes on, each impossibly tall, some spiraling, smooth, and white, others thin and misshapen, as if they'd been drawn into existence by a two-year-old with a pencil. A few were akin to plant-life more than actual buildings, resembling thin, elongated, multicolored pumpkins more than anything else he could think of for comparison.

Next to the city was a lush, green canopy of rather thick-looking jungle, also about 5 miles wide, he guessed. And next to the jungle was another section of land consisting of very tall, very pointy mountains.

Neighboring the mountains was a desert. Julian could see six or seven enormous pyramids, some larger than others, outlined against the horizon. In the middle of the cluster stood the largest of the pyramids, the very tip of which was detached. And floating. Julian squinted, attempting to make out what was moving on the surface of the detached tip. *Is that an eyeball?*

Julian knew immediately what he was looking at; this was the pyramid famously depicted on the back of every dollar bill he'd ever seen, the source of countless conspiracy theories and myths. Which meant that the eyeball set into the floating piece at the top was the all-seeing eye of the Illuminati. Julian had often wondered where the pyramid was actually located.

Well, now I know, he thought with a shrug.

Each section of land was vastly different from the last. This pattern continued around the entire shoreline.

"What are all those places around the edge of the water?" Julian asked the captain, breaking the silence. "It's like there's a different place every way I look."

"Well, when a sleeper dreams of something that happens in a desert, they wind up over there," the captain said, pointing toward the pyramids. "And if they have a dream that takes place in a jungle, they end up over there." He pointed toward the jungle. "And if they dream of being in a—"

"So basically," Julian interrupted, "those are all the places that sleepers go when they have their dreams, and where they end up depends on what they're dreaming about?"

"Exactly!" The captain grinned. His golden teeth glistened. "And whenever a sleeper dreams of a new place, a place no one's ever dreamed of before, all the different lands out there move over and make room for it. That's how Dream keeps gettin' bigger all the time. I'm told things work much the same way in Nightmare, as well," he added.

"Where exactly is Nightmare, anyway?" Ashlynne asked. "Can we see it from here?"

"I'm afraid not," answered the captain. "But if you travel far enough away from the sea in any direction, past the dreamlands that surround us, eventually you reach the twilight; the place where the sky grows dark. And if you go any further, past the twilight, you find yourself in Nightmare. But I wouldn't recommend goin' there. Nightmare's a terrible place, full of evil, dangerous things. And if you stay too long, the fear and sadness will slowly drive you mad, 'till you forget how to be happy altogether. And that's when the Nightmare King's got you."

Julian shivered. He didn't want to see Night-mare or go anywhere near it. Dream was weird enough. He decided to change the subject. "So where do people—I mean sleepers—go when they have a dream about being on water? Wouldn't they be in the water all around us, like the flying people up there?" he asked, gesturing toward the sky. The majority of flying sleepers were behind them now, though a good number who'd strayed from the main party still zoomed and swooped nearby. Julian briefly wondered if they were per-haps curious, like when dolphins follow ships in the ocean.

The captain's dark eyes scanned the skies. "For some reason, the flyin' sleepers usually stay togeth-er, in a big group over the sea," he answered. "No one's yet figured why. But most other dreams are fairly spread out. You don't run into one very of-ten. There's always more room, you see."

Julian just smiled and nodded. The conversations here kept getting weirder and weirder.

"Captain, I was wondering, what's your name?" Ashlynne asked. "We already told you ours, but what about yours?"

The captain smiled at her. "But I already told you my name. It's The Captain. First name *The*, last name *Captain*. But nobody calls me The. Me' friends all call me Captain."

"Oh, I see." Ashlynne said. She looked at Julian and smiled slightly, the corners of her mouth twitching, as if she was stifling a laugh.

Julian smiled back, also doing his best not to laugh, as he didn't want to insult The Captain, who seemed quite proud of his name.

A moment later, Julian was startled by a splash just a few yards from the ship. He watched with fascination as a young woman's head and shoulders suddenly breached the water, her impossibly long hair slowly bobbing to the surface around her, surrounding her in an immense web of colorful locks. Julian couldn't believe how long her hair was. If a strand of it was stretched out in a straight line, he mused, it would probably be about ten times longer than he or Ashlynne were tall. Maybe even longer. He approached the side of the ship and leaned forward over the railing, peering into the water beneath the woman, where a large, glimmering tail-fin swayed steadily back and forth. "Ashlynne look, a mermaid!"

Ashlynne ran over. "Her hair is so pretty," she mumbled next to him after a moment, sounding almost dazed.

She was right—the mermaid's hair was beautiful. It seemed to be every color at once, all blended together, just like the clouds they'd passed through earlier.

"How long do you think it would take someone to grow their hair that long?" Julian asked.

Ashlynne slowly shook her head, mouth agape. "I don't know," she answered. "Probably a hundred years, at least."

"Aye," added The Captain in a hushed voice

from the helm behind them. "I'd say that's about right."

When the pretty young mermaid noticed the three of them admiring her, she smiled and waved. A moment later she stopped waving and cocked her head to the side, as if she'd heard something, her smile contorting into an entirely different face; the skin on her forehead and cheeks sagged as her eyes seemed to melt away, leaving behind hollow, dark pockets of flesh. Her teeth grew into long, sharp-looking fangs, reminding Julian of a vampire's teeth, except every single tooth was pointed, not just the two in the corners. He shuddered and turned away, closing his eyes. He hoped the mermaid would be gone when he opened them back up.

It worked. When he looked back, the mermaid was gone.

He was just about to ask if anyone else had seen the mermaid's face change when a gigantic fish suddenly crashed through the surface of the water a couple of miles off, soaring through the air. A half-second later, an enormous pair of jaws came roaring out of the water beneath it. The massive jaws opened and clamped shut around the poor fish with lightning speed, swallowing it whole. And then the jaws were gone, disappearing back down into the untold depths of the sea.

"Whoa!" yelled Julian. "Ashlynne, did you see that? That thing was *huge*!" He turned to The Captain. "What *was* that thing? Some kind of sea monster or something?"

The Captain's face was white as a ghost. It looked like he couldn't believe what he'd just seen. "Aye," he answered solemnly. "I believe it was, lad."

"And that mermaid," Julian added, "her face . . . it *changed*. Right before she swam away, it twisted up and got all ugly! Did you guys see that?"

"Yeah!" said Ashlynne, her eyes wide. "I saw that too!"

The Captain nodded slowly. "It's the Nightmare King's monsters," he said after a moment.

"Ever since King Morpheus went missin', there've been more of 'em sneakin' into Dream than ever before."

❖

As THEY SAILED along, Julian spotted a small island about a half-mile away from the ship. The island's surface, which was no more than a mile long, was covered by a dense forest. The trees of the forest were colossally tall, with immensely thick trunks, and branches overflowing with rose-red leaves. Julian and Ashlynne had gone on vacation in California when they were seven years old, and they'd seen some big redwood trees that looked very similar to these.

As Julian admired the size of the trees and the mesmerizing, deep red of the leaves, he was surprised to see a very, very tall man suddenly lumber out from the forest onto the island's sandy shore. The man wore only a pair of tattered-looking black shorts; he reminded Julian of a punk-rocker from the 1980s. He had a green, spiked mohawk, a silver hoop-ring through the middle of his nose, and his entire body was covered in dark, elaborate-looking tattoos. He was at least as tall as a two-story house.

"What's that place, over there?" Julian asked, pointing toward the large man and the island.

"That's the Land of Joking Giants, if I'm not mistaken," said The Captain.

"Who's that big guy?" asked Ashlynne.

"Do you know him?" chimed in Julian.

The Captain chuckled. "No, I don't believe I do."

The large man suddenly squatted down in the sand, and picked up what appeared to be a rock, or perhaps a large sea shell. Then he stood and heaved the object into the sky, barely missing a blonde-haired girl who'd been flying above him on a huge winged banana. The giant slapped his knee and stomped with joy, bellowing with laughter, the deep bass of his voice echoing across the sea. Then he bent forward and picked up another object, targeting a different sleeper this time. He missed yet again, erupting into a fresh bout of knee-slapping laughter. Stewie, who lay between Julian's feet, perked up his ears and growled.

Julian frowned. "He looks scary."

The Captain nodded. "Aye. The giants are usually quite friendly, but they are indeed scary-lookin'. And their jokes are awful."

"Awful jokes . . . like mean jokes?" Ashlynne asked.

"No, they're just not funny. And they don't stop talkin', even after it's clear you're not amused."

As the island and the tall, jovial figure slowly faded from view, Julian wondered about the jokes that the giants told. How could someone tell a joke that wasn't funny? If a joke wasn't funny, then in Julian's opinion it wasn't even a joke. It would be more like a riddle or something. Or maybe a prank. And who decided whether or not your jokes were funny, anyway? The joke police? Joke telling was one of Julian's favorite things to do. Was it possible that *he* could be an unfunny joke teller, as well? After a moment of intense consideration on this matter, he decided there was no way that could possibly be true. His jokes were the best. His dad had told him so. And Julian's dad would never lie—especially not about something so important.

"Captain, where are we going, anyway?" Ashlynne inquired.

It was a good question. "Yeah, where *are* we going?" asked Julian. "Are we going to start looking for those blankets soon, or what?" He was getting impatient with all this boring sailing. He just wanted to find those blankets and get out of here. This place was starting to give him the creeps. Plus, there were a whole bunch of video games he'd gotten for his birthday that he couldn't wait to try out.

"We're headed for Dragon Jungle," The Captain said, pointing toward the jungle section of surrounding shore. "We need to start lookin' somewhere for the blankets. And I'm hopin' maybe one of the dragons snatched 'em out of the air when you two arrived, and brought 'em in there. You never know what a dragon might do. Unpredictable beasts, they are." The Captain released his grip on the helm, cupping his hands to his mouth. "Drop anchor and ready the raft, men!"

"Arr!" yelled the leprechauns—in a very piratey way—from their various stations across the ship.

Julian smiled at his sister. "See, Ashlynne? They're going to help us! We'll be home in no time!"

Julian was trying to be brave, but now that he'd seen that scary-looking mermaid, and then that sea monster, he wasn't sure how much longer his bravery would last. This place obviously wasn't as harmless as he'd initially believed. What if something went wrong? What if they wound up stuck here, in this dream place, forever?

V

ONCE THE LEPRECHAUNS had finished lowering their anchor, a rope ladder was hung over the side of the ship, and the small boat that would transport them all to shore was dropped into the water.

Julian approached the railing, expecting to see a customary wooden raft floating below. He looked down and laughed. "Is that . . . is that *toast*? You guys are so weird." It was by far the largest piece of toast he'd ever seen. "How are we supposed to sail on that?"

"Got a problem with our toast, sonny?" snarled blind Jerry, who'd been standing nearby. He was facing slightly to the left, seemingly unsure of Julian's precise location.

"Um, no," stammered Julian. "I ... I just thought that—"

Jerry interrupted Julian with a loud snore, apparently sleeping while standing up again. Julian and Ashlynne exchanged a look and giggled.

The Captain swung his legs over the railing and began his descent down the rope ladder, it's bottom rung hanging just above the toast. Julian, then Ashlynne, and then the rest of the men followed.

Once everyone was safely seated aboard the toast, a few of the leprechauns hoisted a white sail up the short wooden mast that stuck out from the middle of the small vessel. Within moments the sail filled with a warm gust of wind, propelling them toward the jungle.

After a minute or two of smooth sailing, the wind stopped blowing and the sail sagged, bringing the toast to a halt midway to shore.

"Stranded. How convenient," Julian said, laying the sarcasm on pretty thick. "So how are we supposed to get to shore now?"

The leprechauns all looked to one another, shrugging and giving off the overall impression of having no ideas.

"Are there any paddles we can use?" asked Ashlynne.

The Captain turned to her, pointing at one of the many badges prominently displayed on his jacket. In the badge's center was a rather unusual insignia; a paddle with a bright red X over it, crossing it out. "No paddles here, darlin'," he said with a grin. "We'll just have to be patient. The wind should pick up again in no time."

Julian didn't have time for patience. He looked toward the sky, at all the people and things flying around. "Excuse me! Hello! Is there anyone up there who can maybe help us out, please?"

The Captain shook his head. "I already told you, lad. The sleepers almost never pay attention to nothin' except what they're dreamin' about. It's useless askin' them for help."

"Well," Julian shot back, "I just thought that since a couple of them saved us when we were falling out of the sky, maybe they might also help us now."

"No boy, I'm tellin' you it's pointless—"

The crowd of dreamers overhead suddenly parted, all at once, reminding Julian of a flock of birds that suddenly changes direction in unison, as if thinking with the same mind. He looked through the circular-shaped opening that formed in the crowd's center and saw the silhouette of a huge dragon circling high above, just beneath the clouds. It suddenly tucked its wings and dove into the opening, heading straight for Julian and his companions, spinning in a slowly rotating spiral as it soared downward. As it neared the bottom of the opening, it spread its wings, slowing its descent like a paratrooper deploying a parachute.

The dragon was enormous. It was so big, Julian

realized, it could probably eat the entire gym at school in one bite, if it wanted to. Its colors were a swirling blend of light and dark shades of green, with a chaotic pattern of purple and orange that stretched from the base of its snake-like neck all the way to its jawline. The combined length of both its wings rivaled that of a football field; Julian watched as the wings waved slowly back and forth, becoming almost hypnotized by their rhythm as the colossal creature centered itself just above the raft, hovering in place. The dragon suddenly reared its head and spread its jaws wide, displaying several rows of jagged teeth.

The leprechauns promptly burst into a panicked frenzy.

"It's gonna eat us!" yelled one of them, hugging the leprechaun nearest him. "It's gonna roast us and eat us! We're all gonna die!"

Julian was not at all surprised to see that it was blind Jerry making most of the commotion. He briefly wondered how the guy even knew that a dragon was anywhere nearby.

The dragon did not attack. Instead, it leaned its massive head forward, letting out a breath of air so strong that the toast's sail instantly filled, and Julian felt his stomach lurch as the toast shot forward at rocket-speed. He quickly dropped, digging his fingers into the toast, holding tight.

A split second later, the water's surface behind them burst open with a spectacular spray. The jaws of a sea monster erupted, clamping shut with radiating force, in the exact spot they'd just been stranded. Julian briefly wondered if these jaws were the same ones they'd seen earlier eating the giant fish, or if there was more than one of the monsters lurking below. He wasn't sure he wanted to know the answer.

"He saved us!" Ashlynne said. "The dragon saved us from that monster!"

AT THAT SAME moment, a group of mermaids were busy relaxing on a large flat rock nearby, just offshore from the jungle. They'd watched with mild curiosity as a considerably large dragon had flown in through the cloud of dreamers and then rescued a group of little sailors from being eaten by a sea monster. The sailors were currently shooting across the water at a very high speed on what appeared to be a rather large piece of toast, heading straight for the jungle shoreline.

The mermaids breathed a collective sigh, resuming their relaxation.

"ASHLYNNE! WE'RE GONNA crash!" Julian could barely hang on to the toast, which was not holding together very well under the current high-speed circumstances. The rough pieces he grabbed onto kept snapping off as the toast skipped across the sea.

"Just hold on tight!" Ashlynne yelled, hanging on next to him, her cheek pressed into the toast's surface, eyes clamped firmly shut. "I don't think there are any brakes on this thing!"

The leprechauns were still yelling and screaming; Julian could barely hear Ashlynne over all the noise they were making.

A sudden howl surprised him, and he glanced over his shoulder, smiling when he spotted Stewie, who seemed to be having an easy time remaining aboard thanks to the un-trimmed nails jutting from his paws, which he'd dug deep into the craft's brittle surface. The little dog was howling with everything he had, seemingly unaware of any apparent danger, his big, floppy ears flapping wildly in the breeze as his tail wagged ferociously.

A moment later the toast smashed into the shore. Unable to withstand such an impact, it was immediately reduced to crumbs as it exploded onto the beach. Everyone was sent flying through the air, landing together in a large pile on the sand.

Once they'd climbed to their feet, brushed off the sand, and rearranged various disheveled articles of clothing, the search party quickly moved on, venturing into the thick jungle that lay ahead.

VI

THE CAPTAIN LED the way as they traveled single file through the maze of trees. Julian was sure to follow as close as possible; he didn't want to get lost around here. Ashlynne was right behind him, with the rest of the leprechauns bringing up the rear.

Julian felt sort of like he was in one of those movies about the Vietnam War that his father liked to watch, where army guys would go on patrol in the jungle. *Except this is* not *Vietnam,* he thought as a group of three little dragons zoomed through the trees nearby, puffing little balls of smoke and fire as they flew after each other.

"So that's why this place is called Dragon Jungle?" he asked. "Cuz of all the dragons?"

"Aye, lad," The Captain said, using his cutlass to chop branches and vines out of the way as he trudged forward. "This jungle's burstin' at the seams with dragons. Sleepers dream 'em up, then after their dream is done and the sleeper is gone, the dragons fly here to stay. You'll never see two that look the same."

Julian saw scores of dragons as they walked. And like The Captain said, none of them looked alike. Some were big. Some were small. Some were covered with spikes. Others had more than one head. One was a shining, chrome-like silver from head to toe, so shiny it hurt Julian's eyes to look at it for more than a couple of seconds.

Stewie barked like mad at the dragons, prompting one of the leprechauns to shove a brown leather shoulder bag into Julian's arms with the terse instructions to "put that noisy little devil in here."

Julian obliged. He slung the bag over his shoulder and scooped up Stewie, placing him gently inside. Stewie curled up at the bottom, panting, quiet now that his view of the dragons had been successfully obstructed.

"Where are the dragons going?" Julian asked The Captain. The dragons were all flying back toward the sea, in the opposite direction of the twins and their friends.

"I haven't a clue," The Captain replied, slashing at a thick tangle of vines blocking their path. "It's near impossible to successfully decipher the motives of a dragon."

"It just seems like they all might be running—or flying, I guess—away from something." Julian paused and thought for a moment. "Sea monsters can't come out of the water, can they?"

The Captain glanced at Julian briefly, mid slash. "I certainly hope not, lad," he answered. After a few more whacks, the vines at last fell away, clearing the path.

Whatever it was, thought Julian as they resumed their forward march, it certainly had the dragons spooked.

"Captain," Ashlynne asked, "I was just wondering; do you know why King Morpheus left Dream? Why was he living next to us, pretending to be called Mr. Morfy?"

The Captain cleared his throat. "Well, lass," he began, "I've only heard rumors about that, I'm afraid. Word is, the Nightmare King recently sent one of his monsters to kidnap the new queen, Aarya. Snatched her right out of bed on her weddin' night, I'm told, as she slept in the king's personal chamber, up in Castle Asteria. And stealin' someone from Asteria isn't easy, mind you. That castle is heavily guarded. And never in the same place twice, neither. *Very* hard to find.

"Anyway, soon after the kidnapping, Morpheus somehow discovered that the queen was sent through a gateway to the Real World. So he just grabs his blankets and chases right after her.

Quite chivalrous of him, of course, rushin' off to save a damsel in distress and all that." The Captain waved his hand dismissively. "But not a second thought for all the dreams here, and what might happen to us after he's gone." He frowned. "Mighty selfish, if you ask me."

"Did you say queen *Aarya*?" Ashlynne asked.

"Aye, lass. I did."

"No *way!* That's our teacher's name—Ms. Aarya!" Ashlynne turned to Julian, eyes wide. "Julian, do you think since Mr. Morfy is actually King Morpheus, that Ms. Aarya might be the lost queen? I mean, it would explain a lot—like why Mr. Morfy moved in where he did. Ms. Aarya's house is only a couple of blocks away! Maybe he knew she was in the area somewhere, but didn't know exactly where to look."

"No way . . . " Julian began, but then he remembered—Ms. Aarya wasn't even their teacher at the beginning of the school year. They were supposed to have the teacher that everyone hoped they didn't get—that Mr. Bipple guy. But Mr. Bipple moved out of town or something after the first day of school, and Ms. Aarya had been his replacement.

Maybe Ashlynne was right.

VII

THE NIGHTMARE KING stood on the balcony of his castle's highest tower, looking on with pride as scores of Deemins, Phantoms, and Ax-Hand Men assembled in the courtyard far below, preparing for the invasion of Dream. Several bonfires dotted the land amidst the mob of raucous creatures, casting a dull, red glow over the gathering.

Beyond the walls of the massive courtyard lay the sprawling domain of Nightmare in all its splendor. Winged beasts of all shapes and sizes prowled the dark skies, occasional streaks of lightning in the storm clouds above illuminating their horrid silhouettes. Smoke and fire dominated the landscape. Scattered across the horizon stood countless towering, misshapen structures—many them engulfed in flames—each a uniquely horrible place of sadness and torture, borne of the sleepers themselves.

The Nightmare King remembered a time when there was only himself and his castle floating in a sea of darkness around the blinding light of Dream. And now look at the place. It was absolutely stunning—and growing steadily larger with each new nightmare. So much horror had been imagined over the eons, he could now barely see Dream's light from his castle. The sleepers had such vivid imaginations, after all, and their nightmares never ceased to amaze him—not since the very beginning.

A long time ago, soon after the realm of Sleep was first created, two domains appeared within its borders: Dream, and Nightmare.

Dream, a place full of bright color and everlasting light, took form in the very center of Sleep. The Nightmare King's brother, Morpheus, was granted sovereignty over this domain.

And the Nightmare King—who'd been known by many different names throughout his long existence—had been graced with the honor to rule over the wonderful, horrible place known as Nightmare, a realm of eternal darkness that manifested beyond the twilight of Dream, on the edge of Sleep.

For what now seemed like an eternity, the Nightmare King had done his best to ignore the pestering fact that he was not the sole ruler of Sleep. He hated to share power with such a fool as his brother Morpheus, and held an even greater hatred for Dream itself—its horrid, eternal light, and the... *happy* things ceaselessly occurring there.

But if everything goes according to plan, he thought with a twisted smile, *I'll be able to smother that light soon enough.*

Finally, after all this time, he'd thought of a way to be rid of Morpheus.

His plan to use his brother's beloved queen as bait had worked perfectly. As soon as Morpheus discovered that the girl had been sent through a gateway to the Real World, the fool had blindly followed, just as the Nightmare King had known he would.

The Nightmare King had then dispatched several shape-shifting monsters into Dream, giving them orders to watch for any sign of King Morpheus, and retired to his beloved dungeons, attempting to figure out a solution to the glaring flaw in his plans; Morpheus would eventually be back. How could he ensure that the Dream King *stayed* gone, forever?

The Nightmare King had thought, and thought, and thought some more. Yet he could not think of an answer to this seemingly insurmountable problem, and soon began to regret acting in such haste.

He'd been almost ready to give up and simply await Morpheus' inevitable return, when the solution he'd been searching for had at last presented itself in the form of remarkably fortunate news, delivered by a spy who'd been disguised as a mermaid; Morpheus' two Blankets of Stars—his only gateways between Sleep and the Real World—had appeared in the sky among the sleepers, along with two children. Two very *awake* children.

The Nightmare King didn't know how these children had come to possess Morpheus' blankets, nor did he care. The only thing that mattered was that the Blankets were here, and Morpheus was not. And without his Blankets, the King of Dreams would be forever stuck in the Real World.

All the Nightmare King had to do now was invade Dream, find those Blankets, and destroy them—then all of Sleep would at last belong to him.

And under his rule, there would be no more sweet dreams for anyone, ever again.

VIII

ASHLYNNE WAS ABOUT to ask for a break from walking when The Captain led the group into a large, circular clearing. She stopped in her tracks, struck by a sudden feeling of déjà vu. She turned slowly, examining her surroundings.

"I've been here before," she said quietly.

Julian and the leprechauns stopped walking and gathered around, staring at her.

"You've been here before?" Julian swiped some hair away from his eyes, revealing a confused expression. "But that's impossible."

"No, really," Ashlynne said, her voice growing in excitement. "I've totally been here before. Have you ever had one of those dreams over and over again? I think they're called recurring dreams, or something like that. I used to have one all the time after I lost my stuffed animals at the beach when I was little. For like a whole year after that, I kept having the same dream, again and again."

"Yeah," Julian said, nodding. "I remember when you lost those."

She ignored him. "In the dream, I'd be walking in a jungle, and I'd have all of them—Roxy, Spotsie, and Ten—with me, in my arms. Then I'd find this big treasure box sitting open in the middle of a random clearing, just like this one. And then I'd put all of them in the box and bury it, with a shovel that just happened to be there behind a bush, and I'd use the shovel to scrape an X in the dirt over where they were buried. Then I'd wake up. It was the same thing every time, and I had that dream a whole bunch of times. And I swear, this is the place. Right where we're standing." She walked over to the middle of the clearing and knelt, inspecting the dirt. "The X is still here!" she said, grinning.

Julian approached, squinting at the X in the dirt, which was quite legible. "Are you serious?" He looked to The Captain with wide eyes. "But how is that possible?"

"This must've been where you had your dream," The Captain said from where he stood at the edge of the clearing. "As I told you before, the places and things that sleepers dream up stay behind."

Ashlynne's heart raced. She felt dizzy. She ran to the tree on the opposite side of the clearing, where she knew the shovel would be waiting behind a bush. Sure enough, it was right where it should be. She grabbed it, ran back to the X, and began to dig.

A few moments later, her shovel struck something hard. She dropped to her knees, brushing the remaining dirt aside with her hands, revealing the lid of a golden box.

With trembling hands, Ashlynne slowly lifted the lid, and there they were: Ten the dog, Spotsie the leopard, and Roxy the dinosaur.

"I can't believe it!" she said, scooping them up. "They're all here!" She hugged them so, so tight as tears rolled down her cheeks.

She closed her eyes, thinking of the day she'd lost them, long ago.

She'd been at the beach with Mom, Dad, and Julian, and she'd brought her three favorite stuffed animals with her, because she brought them everywhere.

Her parents had offered to walk with her and Julian down to the water, so she'd kissed all three of them on their heads, promising she'd be right back. Then she walked away, leaving them all sitting there on her big pink beach towel.

When she returned from playing in the water, her towel was still in the same spot, but her friends were all gone. Ashlynne cried so hard that it gave her a stomachache and a headache at the same time. Her parents searched everywhere, all over the beach, but they never found Ten, Spotsie, or Roxy anywhere. It was the saddest day of her entire life.

And now here she was, holding them again, reunited at last. Ashlynne couldn't remember ever being as happy as she was at that exact moment.

Julian knelt beside her, peering into the open treasure box. "Whoa!" he said, reaching into the box with both hands. A moment later he pulled out two golden swords.

Skeptical, Ashlynne raised an eyebrow. She was fairly certain the box had been empty once she'd removed her stuffed animals a moment ago. She noticed that each sword had a small letter engraved into the base of its blade. "Look," she said, pointing. "This one has an *A* on it, and that one has a *J*."

Julian inspected the engravings, nodding in approval. "They must be for us," he said, handing her the one marked with an *A*.

Ashlynne reached out and took it, still embracing her stuffed animals with her other arm. "And it's not too heavy, either," she said, turning it over in her hand, studying the smooth, expertly crafted blade. "I don't remember any swords from my dream, though."

"Who cares?" Julian said, slashing the empty air. "They're so awesome!"

"A worthy treasure, indeed," The Captain said, nodding. "But I must remind you, we need to find those blankets as soon as possible. We should really be movin' along now." Without another word, he and his men turned and walked away into the brush past the clearing.

Julian hung his sword from a belt loop on the side of his pants. Ashlynne did the same, and together they hurried after the leprechauns.

IX

"CAPTAIN, WHERE ARE all the dragons?" For some time now, Ashlynne hadn't seen any. There had been so many of them earlier, but now the jungle was empty, quiet, still.

Before The Captain could answer, a faint rumbling, whining sound echoed through the trees. It sounded to Ashlynne like a police car siren approaching from a distance, only with some extra bass.

"What's that noise?" she asked.

The Captain stopped and turned, facing the group, squinting past them into the distance. "I can't be sure." He shook his head. "It could be anything. We best keep pressin' forward. Keep your eyes peeled for anything unusual."

"Anything *unusual?*" said Julian. "This whole place is unusual!"

After a few moments, the rumbling and whining was no longer just a noise; it was now accompanied by a growing tremor in the earth. Something big was coming.

I just hope it's not one of those monsters from Nightmare, thought Ashlynne with a shiver, recalling what The Captain had told her. She took a deep, shaky breath, then approached Julian and began shoving her stuffed animals into his bag alongside Stewie.

"What are you doing?" Julian asked, turning to face her.

"Something's coming," Ashlynne said, a slight tremble in her voice. "We might need to run away. I don't want to drop them. There's enough room next to Stewie."

Julian nodded. "Okay." His voice was shaking,

too.

The rumbling sounds had given way to deep, crashing thuds and booms. The siren noise was now nearly deafening. Yet still, nothing could be seen.

Great, thought Ashlynne, *what is it—an* invisible *monster?*

Suddenly, a large number of small, hairless creatures with enormous feet and red, tear-streaked faces erupted from the brush beneath the trees ahead, each wearing only what appeared to be a diaper. Wailing in apparent terror, they were heading straight for the twins and leprechauns.

"Big-foot Babies!" yelled one of the leprechauns. "It's a stampede!"

"Get up in the trees! Quickly!" bellowed The Captain.

The leprechauns scrambled into the branches of nearby trees, but Julian and Ashlynne stood frozen in place. Ashlynne was somewhere between confused and scared. She guessed Julian felt the same way.

"Hurry!" The Captain yelled a moment later.

Ashlynne snapped back to the moment. She grabbed Julian's arm, yanking him toward the nearest tree. They quickly pulled themselves up into the branches, barely avoiding the first of the babies as it charged past below their dangling feet.

The stampede of Big-foot Babies soon thinned, and was eventually past. The jungle was quiet once more. As the dust settled, everyone began climbing down from the trees.

Ashlynne jumped down, landing on her feet. Julian followed.

"Well *that* was awesome," Julian said, dusting himself off. "Screaming babies with huge feet. Where the heck did they come from?"

The Captain jumped down, landing a few feet away. "Someone dreamed 'em up, long ago," he explained. "They live in Lavender Fields, just beyond the jungle. I've never seen one venture anywhere else before." He paused for a moment, scratching at the dusting of red stubble along his chin. "Somethin' clearly had 'em all worked up."

Ashlynne laughed. "Well *that's* an understatement. Maybe they were chasing the dragons. Or maybe they were all running together, away from something else."

"Who knows," Julian said. "It could be anything in this place. Are we gonna keep going in that direction, even though everything else is headed the other way?"

"Aye," The Captain answered. "We need to search everywhere we can think of for the blankets. We'll cross the bridge to Lavender Fields and have a look around. If we don't find nothin', then we'll turn around and head back, try searchin' somewhere else. We don't want to get too close to Nightmare."

Ashlynne didn't like the sound of that. "How close to Nightmare are we going to get, exactly?"

"The border's just beyond the fields. But don't worry, lass. We won't be gettin' any closer to it than we need to."

X

AFTER PASSING THE last of the trees in the jungle, Ashlynne found herself standing before an enormous canyon. On the opposite side of the canyon lay fields of long, swaying purple grass that stretched for as far as she could see in either direction. A nearby bridge appeared to be the only way across.

"So that must be Lavender Fields," she said, turning to The Captain. "That's where those crazy babies came from, right?"

He nodded. "Yep."

A small wooden sign stuck out of the ground next to the bridge's entrance. Ashlynne approached the sign and knelt, picking dirt off the words that were etched in. "Beware the cracks of Sidewalk Bridge," she read.

"Sounds like advice worth followin'," The Captain said from behind her.

She stood and stepped past the sign, stopping short of the bridge's entranceway. Upon closer inspection, Ashlynne found that it was indeed a sidewalk, judging by the successive narrow sections of rectangular, flat concrete. There were no safety railings or walls on the sides, no curb, and no street—just the sidewalk—and its surface was thoroughly blanketed with a layer of thick, green, wet-looking grime.

Several very tall streetlights were stationed along the sides of the walkway, one every twenty or thirty yards. Many of the posts were slightly crooked, leaning either to the left or right, some leaning at more acute angles than others. Clusters of long, thick, tangled green vines hung from the tops of the lights, swaying softly in the warm breeze. Ashlynne took a step sideways toward the edge of the canyon and peered below the bridge, finding no supporting beams of any kind beneath it. "Do you think it's safe to cross?' she asked.

"Aye," said The Captain, stepping forward. "So long as none of us steps on a crack."

"Is it just me, or is it getting darker out?" said Julian as he approached, squinting toward the sky. He shook his head, seemingly confused. "How is that even possible? I don't see a sun anywhere."

"It gets darker as you get closer to Nightmare," The Captain explained. "But those lights are on." He pointed toward the dimly glowing streetlights looming over the bridge. "We should be able to see well enough. Let's go."

As Ashlynne followed The Captain onto the bridge, she was extra careful not to step on any of the cracks that separated the sections of sidewalk. This proved difficult, however; the slime and mud covering the bridge's surface made the cracks extremely hard to see, especially in some of the extra-mucky spots.

Neither Ashlynne nor any of her companions spoke as they carefully made their way across the bridge, each of them intensely focused on successfully avoiding every last crack.

When they were about halfway to the other side, Ashlynne spotted a small, orange and pink dragon perched on top of a streetlight, not too far ahead. She waved. "Hi! Have you seen any blankets around?"

The dragon looked down at her, made a noise that was somewhere between a squawk and a roar, then spread its impressively colorful wings and lifted off. It flew over their heads, back toward the jungle behind them. Ashlynne sighed, and kept walking.

Before long, everyone in the group was standing safely on the opposite side of the bridge—all except for one leprechaun, who'd fallen a bit behind. Of course, it was Jerry.

And he was snoring.

"Oh no," exclaimed one of the leprechauns. "Jerry's sleepwalkin' again!"

"Someone's got to wake him up, or he'll step on a crack!" said The Captain, eyes wide.

Jerry shuffled along, swaying slightly, taking short, halting steps. Ashlynne couldn't believe he'd managed to avoid all the cracks so far while walking like that.

"What happens when you step on one of the cracks?" she asked.

Before anyone could answer, one of the leprechauns picked up a baseball-sized stone off the ground. "Here, this oughta wake him," he said with a confident sneer, then threw the rock at Jerry.

The stone bounced off Jerry's forehead, causing him to stagger backward. Everyone gasped and went silent, watching in horror. After a few seconds of breathless tension, Jerry let out a fresh snore, resuming his wavering march forward, apparently still asleep.

The Captain cupped his hands around his mouth. "Jerry, you've got to wake up! Don't step on a—"

But it was too late. Jerry's next step was directly on a crack. The sections of sidewalk on each side of the crack instantly crumbled away, and Jerry was gone.

"No!" bellowed The Captain. "Jerry!"

Suddenly, a loud snore echoed out from the canyon beneath the bridge. Five or six of the leprechauns scurried alongside the cliff to the left and right of the bridge's entrance, peering underneath.

"He's there!" one of them reported.

"He's danglin' by his hook!" yelled another. "He didn't fall!"

Ashlynne walked to the edge of the cliff beside the bridge to investigate, and sure enough, there was Jerry, hanging there by the hook that served as his left hand, the unblinking eyes stitched into his patches staring lifelessly as he snored away. Jerry's hook had apparently caught onto the crumbling cement ledge before him as he began to fall, rescuing him from a deadly descent into the rocky canyon.

"Hang on Jerry!" The Captain sprang forward. "I'm coming to save you!" He sprinted onto the bridge, hopping over the cracks. When he arrived at the spot where Jerry had fallen through, he dropped to his knees and reached down, grabbing Jerry with both hands. A moment later, grunting and cursing, The Captain hauled his shipmate up to safety, both of them collapsing backward onto the grimy sidewalk. Jerry continued to snore.

The Captain began gently slapping Jerry's face until he at last appeared to stir, then together they climbed to their feet. Thoroughly caked in sidewalk slime, the pair carefully navigated the remainder of the bridge into the waiting arms of the leprechauns.

"Let's hear it for Jerry, the *sleepin' dangler!*" yelled one of the crew, the others celebrating like a baseball team that just won the big game, jumping up and down, yelling and hollering. They hoisted Jerry up like a crowd surfer at a rock concert as the leprechaun threw a fist into the air, letting out a savage war cry amid their enthusiastic cheers.

Ashlynne couldn't help but laugh. "These guys are nuts," she said to Julian, who stood nearby, laughing with her.

"Yup," he said, nodding and flashing a grin.

Once the leprechauns finished celebrating, the band of searchers pressed onward, into the soft twilight of Lavender Fields.

XI

FIREFLIES BLINKED ALL around them as Ashlynne and her brother walked with their friends through the tall purple grass, a chorus of softly chirping crickets providing a soothing background rhythm to the mesmerizing show of light. Sidewalk Bridge was far behind now, and the further they walked, the darker it became.

The group no longer traveled single file now that they were out of the jungle. The leprechauns had split up and spread out across the field, each of them carefully studying the landscape for any sign of the elusive blankets.

The Captain stopped suddenly at the crest of

a shallow hill, just a few yards ahead of Ashlynne and Julian—who'd been walking side by side for some time now—and knelt in the grass. Everyone stopped, following his lead. After a moment he looked back toward them, placing a finger over his lips. "Shhh," he said, then waved them over.

Everyone raced up the hillside.

Ashlynne reached The Captain first. She knelt next to him, out of breath and panting. Hill sprints were not something she'd planned for. "What is it—" she began, but the words froze in her mouth as her gaze fixed on a large herd of the most beautiful creatures she'd ever laid eyes on.

"Unicorns!" Ashlynne gushed, jumping up and clapping her hands. "And they have wings!" There had to be at least fifty of them, just standing around, eating the grass.

"Shh! You'll spook 'em!" hissed The Captain. "They'll fly away!"

"Sorry!" she whispered, kneeling back down.

"Why are they sort of purple like that?" asked

Julian quietly as he crouched next to them.

"There are unicorns of just about every color," The Captain explained in a hushed voice. "It depends on what kind of grass they like to eat. There's red ones, green ones, orange ones; these ones here clearly like the purple grass." He paused, eyeing Ashlynne and her brother. "I'd wager that if the two of you ate nothin' but purple grass, your skin would eventually turn purple, as well."

Stewie suddenly poked his head out of Julian's bag, ears perked up. He spotted the unicorns and flashed his teeth, growling.

"Shh! Be quiet Stewie!" whispered Julian.

Stewie obediently stopped growling and licked Julian's arm, then disappeared back into the bag.

"Look! There's a baby one!" Julian said, pointing to a little unicorn which was roughly knee-high in comparison to the others. It galloped in tight circles, jumping and flapping its wings, but not lifting off.

Ashlynne gasped, covering her mouth with her

hand. "Oh my god, it's trying to fly! That's so *cute!*"

She' d just finished her sentence when Julian suddenly jumped up. "Look!" he said, pointing toward the hills beyond the unicorns. "The blankets! I think I see them!"

Ashlynne squinted, searching the landscape. The twilight of the fields made it tough to see anything more than about a hundred yards away, reminding her of playing at the park back home at the end of the day during the summer, when the sun has gone down but there's still enough light left over to have fun for just a few more minutes. Ashlynne's eyes welled up, and she immediately shook her head, focusing on the present.

After a moment, she spotted the blankets. On the horizon was a massive tree, the only one in the entire field. She'd been so excited about the unicorns that she hadn't even noticed it. The leaves on the tree were all yellow, save for two dark, sparkling areas that appeared to be fluttering slightly in the breeze.

"I think you're right!" she said. "That might be them!" She stood and started down the hill toward the unicorns, in the direction of the yellow tree. "Let's get over there before they blow away again," she called over her shoulder. "I don't know about you, Julian, but I'm ready to go home!"

Spooking the unicorns no longer a concern, Julian and the others stood and hurried after her.

Several unicorns suddenly began to gallop straight toward her, snorting and neighing loudly.

Ashlynne stopped in her tracks, heart racing.

Are they attacking?

Her fears quickly subsided as one by one the unicorns began to spread their wings and lift off, soaring overhead. The remainder of the herd followed suit a moment later.

As the last of the magnificent animals disappeared over the ridge of the hillside, Ashlynne realized that unicorns were much larger than any horse she'd ever seen—at least twice the size, if not bigger.

"They were so beautiful!" she said, beaming.

"Aye," grumbled The Captain as he trudged past, "but not exactly the friendliest creatures in the world."

At that moment, a bolt of lightning flashed across the darkened skies ahead, briefly illuminating the yellow tree and the shimmering blankets caught in its branches. A far-off rumble of thunder soon followed.

"Is that ... Nightmare?" Julian asked timidly. " ... ahead of us, where it's dark?"

"Aye, lad," The Captain answered, nodding. "That's it alright."

As the group continued onward, faint, distant screeches began to echo all around them.

Ashlynne scanned her surroundings. The fields appeared empty. "Captain, what are those noises?" she asked nervously, the shrieks and cries growing louder with each passing second.

"Those be screamin' Deemins," he answered.

"I'd know that sound in 'me sleep." He stopped walking and turned to his men, pulling his sword from its sheath and raising it high. "Ready your swords, lads!" he snarled. "We need to get to those blankets, no matter what gets in our way!" He turned and began sprinting toward the tree.

The leprechauns erupted in a war cry, drawing their swords and rushing after him, pushing past Ashlynne and Julian.

"Come on Ashlynne, let's go!" said Julian, and they both began to run.

After a moment, Julian—who'd always been the better runner—was beginning to pull ahead. "Ashlynne, you have to run faster!" he called over his shoulder. "If we lose those blankets again, we might never get back home!"

"I'm trying!" she called back, unable to mask the desperation in her voice. "I'm going as fast as I can!"

After what seemed like forever, they at last reached the tree. It stood at the crest of a hill, beyond which lay a narrow valley, followed by yet another gently sloping hillside.

The lowest branches of the tree were too high for any of them to reach, and Ashlynne had just been about to ask how they were supposed to get way up there when The Captain suddenly barked an order.

"Beemos, Braxton, fetch the blankets!"

Two of the nearest leprechauns, each sporting a dark-green top hat and a curly, handle-bar mustache, nodded solemnly. They launched into the air, landing high up in the branches, right near the blankets.

"Whoa!" Ashlynne and Julian said, simultaneously.

"How are they jumping like that?" Ashlynne asked. "Captain, can you do that too?"

He grinned at her. "Yes, my lady. Jumpin's what leprechauns do best."

"Ya, I guess so!"

The two strikingly similar-looking leprechauns

snatched the blankets from the branches and jumped to the ground, landing hard with a *thud*.

As they handed the blankets to The Captain, Ashlynne spotted a growing number of small, black shapes appearing in the skies on the horizon beyond the tree. Shapes with large, dark wings.

"What's that?" she asked quietly, pointing.

The Captain looked to where she pointed, squinting. "It's the phantoms," he said after a moment. "We need to go. Now."

Suddenly, a hoard of enormous, dark creatures emerged over the ridge beyond the valley. They charged down the slope, heading straight for Ashlynne and her friends.

The giant monsters shrieked and screamed as they tore through the tall grass, each the size of a two-story house and pitch-black from head to toe, their long, pointed teeth foaming with spit and drool. They reminded Ashlynne of a movie she'd once seen about evil, mutated rats that ran around attacking everyone—except these things were much bigger than rats. And there were men, or what looked like men, standing sideways on the backs of the colossal rat creatures, balancing like surfers from hell. And they appeared to be holding weapons.

"It's the Deemins!" The Captain snarled. "And what the devil are those things ridin' on 'em?"

"Those guys don't have hands!" said Julian, his face white as a ghost.

"Oh no . . . they have axes for hands." Ashlynne was so scared her voice barely came out.

"Ax-Hand Men!" shouted one of the leprechauns, his words laced with fear.

"How do you know they're called Ax-Hand Men?" asked another.

"Well, they have axes instead of hands, so I just thought—"

"So you just thought they must be called *Ax-Hand Men?* First of all, there's no way they're called Ax-Hand Men. That's a ridiculous name. And second—"

"Quiet down, you fools!" The Captain interrupted. "It doesn't matter what they're called. Let's just go get 'em!"

❧

THE LEPRECHAUNS RAISED their swords high and cheered as The Captain approached Julian, shoving the blankets into Julian's arms. "Take these, and run that way! Both of you!" he said, pointing his sword in the direction of Sidewalk Bridge. "Get back across the bridge, and do your best to reach the jungle before those phantoms get here. Then you need to find a place to hide so you can fall asleep under the blankets. We'll hold the monsters back for as long as we can. Now go!"

Julian watched as each of the leprechauns, including The Captain, suddenly launched incredibly high into the air, so high that they disappeared into the clouds. They reemerged a moment later, screaming down through the sky feet first, yelling

and howling like madmen. One by one they landed on the backs of the charging Deemins, flat-
tening the beasts like pancakes, reducing them to
nothing more than large, black, oily-looking
splotches on the hillside. The Ax-Hand Men who
rode them tumbled away into the purple grass,
seemingly unharmed.

Julian was impressed with the leprechauns'
show of force, but they were vastly outnumbered.
He wasn't sure how long they'd last—and the
phantoms hadn't even arrived yet, their dark forms
growing ever larger as they approached from beyond the hills.

Julian averted his gaze from the phantoms.
With trembling hands, he stuffed the blankets into his bag alongside Ashlynne's treasure and
Stewie, who was somehow still sleeping in spite of
all the commotion. Then he ran to Ashlynne, who
stood with her mouth hanging open, watching the
battle unfold.

"Come on," he said, grabbing her arm and

pulling. "Let's go!"

Without another word, they turned and ran as the grotesque shapes of the phantoms began to fill the skies overhead.

XII

"**H**URRY ASHLYNNE! RUN!**" Julian yelled over the deafening screeches of the deemins as he and Ashlynne made their way up the slope of a particularly steep hill.

As they neared the top, at least a hundred unicorns suddenly burst over the ridge directly before them with a powerful rush of wind, flying low, their hooves just a few feet overhead as they passed.

Julian and Ashlynne stopped running and turned to watch them. After a moment, Julian realized that although many of the unicorns were varying degrees of purple, most of the others were not; he could make out distinct shades of red, yellow, blue, orange, and green among the airborne herd.

"The unicorns!" Ashlynne shouted, grinning. "They came back!"

"I don't think those are the same unicorns," said Julian, squinting into the dim light. "Look at their colors. There's only a few purple ones. The rest are all different."

"Wow," said Ashlynne. "You're right. And they're all big. I don't see any of the smaller ones or babies."

Julian shrugged. "Maybe those are the warrior unicorns. It looks like they might be getting ready to fight."

The unicorns spread out and slowly ascended, silently approaching the dark forms of the phantoms from below. As the unicorns closed in, the tips of their horns began to glow, emanating a dull, opaque blue that quickly became so intensely bright Julian was almost forced to look away, but at the last moment the horns erupted with light, emitting thick beams of blinding blue, instantly vaporizing several phantoms into clouds of black mist.

The phantoms, whose vast numbers now seemed to almost fill the sky, began to fight back, impossibly long trails of fire spewing from their mouths toward the unicorns.

Beams of light and trails of fire streaked back and forth across the heavens as they fought, the unicorns bobbing and barrel-rolling their way through the swarming mass of phantoms.

For a few moments the unicorns appeared untouchable, until a phantom managed to catch hold of a green unicorn's wing. The unicorn let out a piercing squeal and tumbled from the sky, entangled in a deadly embrace with the dark monster, the phantom biting and clawing at its side. In that instant a blue unicorn suddenly swooped in and blasted the phantom into nothing. The green unicorn spun away, spreading its wings and returning to the fight above, a prominent red gash glistening along the side of its neck.

In that moment, a yellow unicorn emerged from the battle, circled down, and landed nearby. It trotted over to Julian and Ashlynne and knelt low, waiting, as if it wanted them to get onto its back.

Julian immediately ran over and climbed on, then turned to find Ashlynne frozen in place, yet again. He rolled his eyes. She was staring at a group of five or six Ax-Hand Men who'd broken through the leprechauns' line of defense and were now were running through the grass with their ax arms swinging, heading straight toward Julian and Ashlynne.

"Come on, we need to hurry Ashlynne!" Julian pleaded, his voice barely audible, drowned out by the ceaseless screams of the few remaining Deemins. She seemed to not hear him. "Ash-lynne," he said, louder this time, "we need to go *now!*"

She shook her head, snapping out of her daze, then ran over and climbed onto the unicorn's back behind him. As soon as she sat down the unicorn stood and began to run. A moment later it spread its wings and they were airborne, ascending high over the fields.

The battle in the sky raged all around them, bursting with light and fire. As their unicorn steed weaved its way through, Julian realized that the phantoms were bigger than the unicorns—but not by much. He managed to catch a few brief glimpses of the dark monsters' faces as they whizzed by, but all he could make out were clusters of black, egg-shaped eyeballs, sticking out like blisters above mouths full of black, jagged, protruding teeth.

Alright, thought Julian, his insides surging with fear, *I want to go home now.*

He held on tight, hugging the unicorn's back as they dipped and spun through the chaos. A fireball suddenly shot past on the right, no more than a foot away, the intense heat of the flame singeing his skin. He looked over his shoulder and saw a phantom trailing a few yards behind, following their every move. It seemed to notice Julian looking at it, and its mouth stretched open wide—too wide—as a deafening, high-pitched screech erupted, sounding like a hundred people dragging their fingernails across a chalkboard in unison.

The noise cut through Julian's thoughts like a knife. His first instinct was to release his hold on the unicorn and cover his ears, but he didn't give in—if he let go, even for a second, he would certainly fall off—so he just shut his eyes tight and clenched his teeth in agony. "Watch out!" he yelled to the unicorn. "Behind us!"

The unicorn swerved to the side just as the phantom unleashed another red-hot stream of fire. It passed on the left, narrowly missing. The unicorn turned upward, spinning upside down in an arch over the pursuing phantom, it's horn beginning to glow.

The phantom attempted to spin out of the way as light shot from the unicorn's horn, striking it square in the chest. It exploded instantly, and they passed directly through the small, dark cloud that had just been the phantom as the unicorn made a tight turn, continuing its flight away from the battle toward the distant jungle.

At that moment, no more than fifty yards ahead, a bright white light flashed just below the clouds. The sky suddenly tore open around the light, forming a void at least a mile wide. A white, sloping wall shimmered into focus within its midst; the wall appeared to be part of a much larger structure hidden from view, possibly a castle.

More than a thousand golden-clad knights riding silver, winged horses came soaring over the wall and through the tear, an entire army pouring into the sky through the void like blood from an open wound. Long red hair spilled from beneath the warriors' helmets, streaming behind like trails of fire.

As the golden warriors swooped past, Julian observed that each of them wore a golden sword attached to their backplate—golden, just like the ones they'd discovered in Ashlynne's treasure box. The warriors began to fight alongside the unicorns, hurling their swords at the horde of demonic phantoms, possessing a seemingly endless supply of the weapons; each time one of them grabbed a sword from their back and threw it, a new sword would instantly appear in the old one's place. Some of the warriors were grabbing and throwing swords in such rapid succession that their arms swirled into a blur, their blades cutting through the sky with the speed of a machine gun spitting bullets, vaporizing the monsters in their path.

Phantoms were exploding into black dust in every direction as the tear in the sky slowly shrank away. Its shimmering, glowing edges morphed and flowed together until it was gone, flashing brightly one last time before blinking out, leaving behind an empty sky.

Julian turned to watch the battle continue to unfold as it slowly faded from view behind them. He could barely make out the leprechauns, who were still busy with the Deemins and Ax-Hand Men down on the ground. They'd stopped jumping and were now fighting with their swords; Julian briefly wondered why. Perhaps they'd grown tired, he decided.

A small group of the red-haired warriors suddenly landed their winged horses among the leprechauns and swiftly dismounted, each drawing a pair of swords and throwing themselves at the surrounding monsters, engaging without hesitation.

"Ashlynne, look!" said Julian. "Those guys are helping the leprechauns!"

"Julian . . ." she responded, "what is that, way over there?"

Julian looked to where her gaze was directed. Far behind the battle, beyond the hills over the dark horizon of Nightmare, a giant, green, glowing cloud was slowly taking form. But it somehow seemed thicker, more substantial than a regular cloud, like oil had been spilled across the sky. And it was huge—it seemed to stretch all the way across the horizon.

But what scared Julian the most were the eyes. The blob had *eyes.* Red, glowing eyes that looked like they were made of fire.

A deep, rumbling sound began to echo across the purple fields. At first it sounded like thunder from a distant storm, but the sound stretched out into what sounded like a voice, saying *GIVE ME THE BLANKETS.*

"Julian, what *is* it?" Ashlynne asked again.

"I don't know," he answered with a shaky voice, his heart in his throat, "but it sounds like it wants the blankets."

As he finished his sentence, an arm with an enormous hand suddenly began to grow out from the middle of the green blob. It slowly wormed forward, oozing across the sky.

It was heading straight for them.

XIII

"ASHLYNNE, LOOK!" JULIAN yelled. "The hand . . . it's coming!"

The green hand had stretched impossibly far, from the distant horizon all the way across the purple fields, appearing to grow larger the further it stretched. It had already snaked around the distant aerial battle, casting a dull, green glow over the action, and Julian could tell by how fast they were flying that if they didn't speed up, it would catch up to them very soon.

Ashlynne looked over her shoulder and screamed. The hand, still growing and stretching, seemed to block out the whole sky now, its wriggling fingers towering overhead like a warped tidal wave, threatening to break at any moment.

Julian had never been so scared in his entire life.

"You need to go faster!" he said to the unicorn over the roaring wind, his voice pleading. "Something's coming, and it's gonna get us!" He turned to look once more, and saw that it was too late. The hand had caught up to them at last.

"Ashlynne!" Julian yelled, drawing his sword. "We need to fight!" There were times to cry and be scared, but this wasn't one of them.

Julian could see the fear in her eyes, but Ashlynne nodded firmly. She grabbed hold of the golden blade's handle at her side, sliding it from her belt loop just as the hand began to close around them.

"Now!" roared Julian, and together they raised their swords, slashing into the hand.

—

There was a blinding flash of light as the sleepers'

swords sank into the Nightmare King's hand. Searing pain coursed through him, and he cried out in agony. How could these children hurt *him?*

And then he realized his futile error. He'd underestimated one small detail; these two were not sleepers. They were *awake.*

Rage coursed through the Nightmare King as he realized his plan had failed. How could he have been so careless? The blankets had been within reach, and now they were gone.

He withdrew his arm and retreated, quickly shrinking away as he resumed a smaller form.

—

"Woo-hoo!" hollered Julian, grinning as he watched the hand fade into the distance. "We did it!"

A moment later the hand was gone, disappearing from view over the hills into the darkness of Nightmare.

The soft dusk light of the purple fields was far behind now as the unicorn dipped low and soared over the treetops of the jungle.

"I know!" Ashlynne said. "I can't believe it! What was that thing, anyway?"

Julian shook his head. "I don't know. But it came from that Nightmare place. Maybe it was a bad dream someone had." He paused as he slid his sword back into the belt loop at his side. "A *really* bad dream."

"I think you call that a nightmare, Julian."

They both laughed, uneasily.

"It's a good thing we had these," said Ashlynne, examining her sword with renewed interest.

"Yeah, no kidding," said Julian. "I hope that thing doesn't come back again." He looked behind them once more, just to be sure it was still gone. He took a deep, soothing breath when he saw nothing but empty skies. "So what do we do now? Just cover ourselves with the blankets and try to fall asleep?"

"I guess so," Ashlynne answered. "That's how The Captain said it would work."

Julian paused, frowning. "Do you think they'll be alright? The Captain, and the other leprechauns?"

Ashlynne smiled. "They seemed pretty tough. Did you see them jumping like that? Plus, those guys with the red hair seemed to be helping them. I'm sure they'll be fine. Let's just go home, okay?"

"Okay," he said, nodding. He removed the blankets from his bag and saw that Stewie was still snoring away in there, curled up with Ashlynne's stuffed animals. Julian smiled down at the little dog as he handed one of the blankets to his sister, and a wave of sadness washed over him. *Goodbye, Stewie,* he thought, eyes welling up. *I'll miss you.*

"Excuse me," Ashlynne said, speaking to the unicorn, "mister, um ... Unicorn, sir? Thank you very much for saving us, but would you mind helping with just one more thing? Could we please go to sleep on your back, while you fly up here? We'd really appreciate it. It feels much safer than going back down there." She glanced toward the jungle below and frowned.

The unicorn neighed and shook its head up and down.

Ashlynne laughed. "I guess that's a yes. Thank you so much!"

And with that, Julian wrapped himself in the shimmering blanket, and Ashlynne did the same. He lay forward, nestling his cheek in the short, silky fur between the unicorn's broad shoulders.

As his sister rested her head on his back, Julian closed his eyes, exhausted, his thoughts quickly quieting, blurring together as he drifted off . . .

XIV

ASHLYNNE OPENED HER eyes. She was staring at a ceiling... a *familiar* ceiling... her *bedroom* ceiling!

I'm home! she thought with a flood of relief. The plan had worked, just as The Captain said it would!

She sat up in bed like a rocket.

She looked at Julian, sleeping in his bed on the other side of the room, and a smile crept across her face. He was covered with one of the Blankets of Stars! She looked down ... so was she! She'd been right—one of their parents must have come in and covered them up during the night, after they'd fallen asleep. She threw the blanket off and jumped out of bed, ran to Julian, grabbed his shoulders, and began shaking him.

"Hey what—" he mumbled, then his head snapped up. He propped himself up on his elbows, smiling as he surveyed his surroundings, clearly relieved. "We're home!" he said, plopping back down onto his back. "We made it."

Suddenly, something rather large began rustling around under Julian's blanket. As the twins watched with eyebrows raised, the lump traveled toward the edge of the blanket. They each gasped as a furry head emerged.

"Stewie!" said Julian. "I can't believe he's here!" The little dog barked then ran across the bed, proceeding to drench Julian's face with slobbery licks as Julian embraced him.

Ashlynne reached down and grabbed the shimmering blanket that covered her brother. She pulled it away, revealing the leather bag he'd carried through Dream, along with his golden sword, which lay on the bed beside his legs.

"Yes! My sword!" He grabbed it by the handle, lifting it. "Look, Ashlynne, your sword's here too!" he said, pointing toward her bed, where her sword lay half obscured by the blanket. "I guess the unicorn was the only thing under the blankets that stayed behind in Dream. Maybe it's because he wasn't sleeping, like us and Stewie," he mused, slowly running his finger along the edge of the blade as it glistened in the morning sunlight. After a moment he carefully laid it back down on the bed beside him.

Ashlynne didn't care about the swords. She was staring at the leather bag, her heart racing. She picked it up and opened the top, holding her breath as she peered inside . . .

"They're here!" she said breathlessly, her hands trembling as she reached into the bag and pulled out Roxy, Ten, and Spotsie. She hugged them, tears streaming down her cheeks. "They're really here! They're really, really here!"

"Ashlynne," Julian said quietly.

She kept hugging her stuffed animals with her eyes closed.

"We need to return these blankets to Mr. Morfy—I mean, King Morpheus."

A FEW MINUTES later, Ashlynne stood with her brother on Mr. Morfy's front porch, each of them clutching one of the blankets. Ashlynne's hands were sweating, and she couldn't seem to stop shuffling back and forth. What if the king was angry? Was he *really* a king? Was *any* of this even real?

Before they'd left their bedroom, Julian hid Stewie and the two swords in their closet while Ashlynne had grabbed a wallet-sized picture of her fourth-grade class from her desk drawer. Pretty red-haired Ms. Aarya was in the picture, standing there smiling next to the class, so Ashlynne stuffed it into her pocket, figuring she'd show it to the king. Maybe he'd recognize her.

Ashlynne reached forward and rang the doorbell. After a moment, the mysterious man who lived there opened his door. He looked down, smiling his familiar, sad smile.

"Hey guys, what are you two doing here so early—" He frowned when he noticed what they were holding. "What are you doing with those?"

They handed him the blankets, and Ashlynne began to explain. She told him everything that happened, from when Fuzzy went missing, all the way to when they woke up this morning, back in their beds under the blankets. The only time Julian spoke was to apologize for taking the blankets without asking first.

When Ashlynne was finally done talking, Mr. Morfy smiled. He hadn't said anything yet to confirm that he was in fact the King of Dream, and for a second she half-expected him to ask if she and her brother had gone completely insane.

"You should never take things that aren't yours

without asking permission," he said, pausing to look each of them thoroughly in the eyes, "and you *certainly* shouldn't be sneaking out at night, even to find your cat. But I won't say anything to your parents about this if you two promise to never do anything like that again."

"We promise," they said, nodding.

"Alright. Well in that case, I'm just happy you both made it home safely. Sleep can be a dangerous place."

Ashlynne gasped. He *was* the king. "Mr. Morfy—I mean, Your Highness... um... there's just one more thing." Ashlynne reached into her pocket and pulled out the class picture with Ms. Aarya. She held it up to show him, and his eyes grew wide.

"Where... do you know where she is?" he asked quietly. He couldn't seem to take his eyes off the picture.

"It *is* her!" Ashlynne clapped her hands and grinned. "I knew it! Ms. Aarya *is* the lost queen!

She lives just a couple of blocks down, on the same street we live on. Julian knows the number of her house. *Don't* you, Julian?"

Julian turned red.

"C'mon, Julian," she said with a sly smile. "He needs to know."

"It's number nine," Julian mumbled, pointing. "Way down that way."

"Julian and his friends always ride their skateboards past Ms. Aarya's house," Ashlynne explained. "They all *looove* her." She began to make kiss noises.

Julian turned even redder. He gave her shoulder a shove, and she laughed.

The King of Dreams smiled. Ashlynne noticed the sad look he usually had was gone. "Thank you both very, very much," he said, "and please, take care of Louie for me."

As if on cue, a distant bark echoed through the open door behind him from somewhere unseen within the house. Ashlynne and Julian exchanged a glance, eyebrows raised.

Without another word, their neighbor walked past them and down the porch steps, still holding the two blankets, and headed in the direction of Ms. Aarya's house.

"Do you think he's going to see Ms. Aarya?" Julian asked, watching him go.

"Yep," Ashlynne said quietly, smiling.

Julian turned and met her eyes, flashing her a big grin. "Want to go to the park?"

"Sure!" she said, then bolted down the porch steps. She turned and headed down the street toward the park at the corner, in the opposite direction of Ms. Aarya's house. "Last one there's a stinky shoe!"

"HEY, WAIT!" JULIAN called after Ashlynne as she ran ahead. He jumped off the porch, skipping all the stairs, then sprinted after her in pursuit. Beyond Ashlynne was their friend Flora, already at the park waiting for them, perched up on the chain-link fence, smiling and waving.

"C'mon, Flora's there!" Ashlynne yelled over her shoulder.

"Hang on, I'll be right there!"

Julian jogged to a halt and turned around. Ms. Aarya's house was in the distance, near the end of the street, and he could see Mr. Morfy standing at her door. He briefly wondered if Mr. Morfy had already rung her doorbell, or if he was maybe trying to build up his courage first, when the door suddenly opened. Ms. Aarya leapt out, hugging Mr. Morfy so hard it sent him staggering backward off her doorstep. Once Mr. Morfy managed to stabilize himself, he kissed her.

After they finally stopped kissing, Mr. Morfy carried her through the open doorway and into the small house. Julian caught a brief glimpse of the sparkling blankets in Mr. Morfy's hand as the door slammed shut.

A moment later, just as Julian was about to head back toward the park, a bright light suddenly flashed from a window near the front of Ms. Aarya's house.

He just smiled and shook his head. He was still having trouble believing any of this was really happening.

After a moment of deep thought on this matter, he turned, and ran off to join his friends.

EPILOGUE

NEITHER MR. MORFY NOR Ms. Aarya were ever seen or heard from again. The mystery behind their disappearance was never solved; it was as if they'd simply disappeared.

Only Ashlynne and Julian knew where they'd gone—and who would ever believe them?